HANNAH

"I AM THE STORM"

D1825940

Paul Rees

Dedicated to 'Podge'

The 'Staffie' who adopted me.

Thank you for the love, loyalty and laughter.

You would have been 'Sav' if you had been taller.

x

When you come out of the storm, you won't be the same person who walked in. That's what the storm is all about.

~Haruki Murakami

Chapter 1.

Homeless.

Dardan Flaka, also known as 'The Boss', sat in his plush office just off George Street in the heart of Manchester.

At six feet six inches tall and weighing in at some 22 stone, Dardan was a bruiser, and his henchmen knew it. He sprawled in a magnificent black leather reclining chair and glared at two of those henchmen. They were also 'bruisers', but not in the same class as Flaka. Granit and Ismet Bektashi stood waiting instructions. They were twins and the only visible difference was the beard that Granit favoured. All three were solid muscle but Flaka possessed brains and guile, something the other two definitely lacked.

Dardan glowered at the twins.

"Well?" he demanded in his deep voice, laced heavily with an Albanian accent, "Have you got her on board yet?"

It was Ismet who took the risk of incurring his boss's wrath by answering,

"No Boss, she won't play ball." His accent was also Albanian but his English was impeccable.

Flaka leaned forward, then, quick as a whippet, slammed his meaty fist on his expensive mahogany desk and shouted,

"Get her to play ball, tonight! I don't care how, just do it! Even if she gets hurt. Understand?"

The twins nodded and, seeing Flaka's nod of dismissal, left the office.

The subject of their conversation was, at that very moment, setting up her space outside a convenience store not far away. She placed her blanket very carefully on the cold pavement, her few possessions which she carried around in two Tesco carrier bags, she placed to one side, then covered them with an old woollen jumper. She thought she might need that later. People walked past her, oblivious to the short waif like girl. Then Hannah sat cross legged, her old tatty skirt covering her knees. The anorak she wore would barely protect her from the evening chill. She hoped to 'earn' enough tonight to get her into one of the only two hostels in the city. Ten pounds for a bed for the night but be gone by nine o'clock in the morning. No breakfast but at least it was warm and dry, if a little dangerous to the unwary.

Settling down, Hannah kept her eyes down but was more

than aware of her surroundings, her years on the streets giving her an innate sense of danger.

She saw the man approaching her from across the road and thought he looked familiar. Her memory was good and she remembered back some three years. Back then the man was with his sixteen-year-old son and they had been kind and generous to her.

'I wonder why he's returned?' she thought, looking straight at him as he got nearer.

The man smiled, a genuine full-face smile, not like most she saw. She smiled back and he approached closer.

He stood in front of her.

"Hello Hannah" he said.

She was surprised that he remembered her name and looked at him quizzically.

He smiled again, "I've never forgotten your name. In fact, I've been back many times, hoping to see you again."

Hannah studied him intensely, relying on her instincts to detect any sign of a problem. There was none. He stood at about six feet two inches tall, slim but with an obvious physique that had been well honed. His stone Chino's and T shirt were clean but obviously not new and the desert boots he wore were clean but well used. His hair was cropped short to his scalp and grey, making him look older than he probably was. Hannah was attracted by his light blue eyes which sparkled at her.

He held out a photo to her which she took. The man was in it, crouching down beside her, she was smiling a radiant smile and he looked happy too. Tears came to her eyes as she held the photo, trembling slightly.

"I remember you taking this. You kept it. Why?"

A sad look came across his face, and his mind went back three years,

"It's a long story" he whispered. "Very long."

Three years earlier.

Two weeks after the Manchester Arena bombing, Greg Angel took his son to Manchester as a birthday treat. Living in Snowdonia, shopping for a growing lad was difficult. No, he wanted to go to a city to buy more trendy clothes and so Greg had made the booking. Then disaster struck and 22 young people were murdered in a terrorist attack. Greg's son, Conner, was undeterred and so the trip went ahead.

Conner had lived with Greg, his father for eight years and they were almost inseparable. The two had driven to Manchester and checked into the 4* hotel, Greg had booked. Conner was suitably impressed. After dumping their bags, they had set off around the shops. For a lunch break, they had visited the display of flowers left as a mark of respect to the fallen. Conner surprised his Father by stopping by every police officer and thanking them for their service. Many officers thanked him for his support, some even had tears in their eyes as they spoke. Greg was full of pride for his boy who was fast becoming a man. However, he was constantly alert, being a former soldier and policeman himself. No harm was going to come to his boy, not while Greg had a breath in his body.

During the afternoon the pair spent more time trawling the shops for Conner. Then they returned to the hotel where Greg had laid on a small surprise. While they sat awaiting their meal, two waiters arrived with a cake, complete with candles, and sang Happy Birthday to a very embarrassed sixteen-year-old. He thanked them and the pair ate their dinner.

"Time to walk off that food mate" Greg said and they walked around Manchester City Centre.

It was as they approached a convenience store that Greg saw Hannah. She sat cross legged with a dirty blanket under her. Her short black hair was dirty and matted, her face pasty, her clothes in need of replacing. Greg stopped and he and Conner observed for a moment.

"Dad" Conner said, "Can we help her?"

Greg looked at the girl. She had an elfin like face, a sad look but when she smiled, her face changed completely. She had potential as a decent human being if given the chance and the support.

Greg nodded, "Come on, we'll ask if we can help."

They crossed the busy road, narrowly avoiding being run over by a silent tram. Then they approached this waif.

"Excuse me" Greg said. "Can we help you?"

The girl looked up and smiled.

"Thank you" she replied, her voice soft.

"Have you eaten today?" Conner blurted out.

The girl looked down but didn't answer. Greg took that to be a 'no'. He turned to Conner,

"Wait here" he said and went into the shop.

Five minutes later he emerged with two carrier bags full of food, sandwiches, pies, pasties, crisps and even chocolate. He'd included several bottles of orange juice and had slipped a ten-pound note into the bottom of one of the bags.

The girl looked at the goods, her face lighting up.

"Oh, thank you!" she said, beaming with joy. "You're too kind."

It was now Greg's turn to be embarrassed. He went slightly red and mumbled something even Conner didn't hear.

"My name is Greg" he eventually managed. "This is my son, Conner."

She looked up, "Hannah" she replied. They shook hands, as

if it were the most natural thing in the world, and Greg squatted beside her. Conner moved off and took a photo of the pair. He had no idea why, it just seemed right.

Greg sat and chatted with Hannah for several minutes. He learned that she had been homeless for six years, having been turned out by her step-father when she rejected his advances. Greg asked about hostels and was told there were only two in the area and they charged ten pounds per night. Greg was appalled. He asked if he could do anything else to help this girl but she declined. She obviously still had some pride so he didn't push it.

As they made to leave, Conner thrust something into Hannah's hand.

"See if you can get the hostel for a couple of nights" he said, backing away before she could refuse.

Tears filled Hannah's eyes as she thanked him. The lad had surprised his father yet again that day. He too felt emotional at what his son had done.

"Can we come back to see you again?" he asked.

"Of course," she replied "But I don't know where I'll be allowed to set up. The police move us on so we don't become part of the furniture!" she chuckled.

Greg and Conner promised to return, which they did for the next two nights but could not find her. They were both disappointed, Conner in particular, as they really felt this young woman needed help and they were hoping to provide that help.

On the Sunday evening, after a last, long look around, the left for home. Neither spoke for a long time in the car. Both wishing they had helped straight away.

Greg decided that he would make every effort to track Hannah down and set about his quest. Working from home as a Security Consultant, he was able to access the internet and placed a search in motion. No one knew of Hannah. His appeal on Twitter met with no response. He contacted the local police but was stonewalled he thought. One officer in particular, Sergeant Davy McReanor, was particularly obstructive which angered both Greg and Conner.

Weeks and months went by with no news. The pair travelled back to Manchester many times over the following three years. But they had their lives to live as well. Conner left college and moved to the Midlands with his job with the NHS. The Covid-19 pandemic arrived and cast chaos across the country, and Greg agreed to adopt an ex-army War Dog.

Sav, apparently shortened from 'Savage' was a nine-year-old German Shepherd who had seen active service in Iraq and Afghanistan with his handler. Now deemed too old to serve, Greg and Conner went to Melton Mowbray to collect him. Both were excited but somewhat apprehensive. They had no need to worry. Sav took to them straight away and travelled home in the back of their Landrover peacefully.

They had been given a list of words of command and antidote words that the dog would obey. Sav was trained to attack and kill on demand. He would defend his new masters with his life if necessary but visitors to their home had to be warned not to raise their voice nor their hands as the dog would growl in warning.

Greg was brought back to the present when he heard a gasp from Hannah. He looked at her, and saw an expression of abject horror on her face. Following her gaze, Greg saw two well-built muscled men crossing the road towards them.

"You'd better go" Hannah whispered, fearing what could happen to this man who had been so kind.

"Friends of yours?" Greg asked.

"No!" she spat. "I hate them."

Greg stayed crouched beside the girl. He studied the men. Both dressed alike, black ill-fitting suits, white shirts and black ties, open at the neck. One had a beard, the other clean shaven.

'Twins' he thought. 'This could be interesting.'

Granit and Ismet walked towards the couple, grinning in anticipation of some fun. As they got nearer, Granit spoke,

"You, old man, fuck off!"

Greg remained where he was, watching their body language. Over confident, anticipation that their mere size would scare him off.

"Hey, old man, I tell you fuck off, NOW!" Granit repeated.

Greg stood slowly and looked at the men.

"Twins?" he asked quietly.

Granit looked at him, a look of surprise registering on his face. That was when Greg knew they would telegraph their moves.

"How you know this, eh?" Granit growled.

"A bit obvious mate. Easy to tell the difference though."

"How?" Ismet spoke, intrigued.

Greg spoke to Granit,

"Your sister doesn't have a beard."

Beside him Hannah gasped again, bringing her hands up to cover her eyes. She whispered,

"You don't know who you are messing with!"

Greg kept his eyes on the men. When the insult finally sank in, Granit let out a roar of anger and stepped forward quickly, hands still by his side.

Greg had studied various aspects of martial arts but decided not to use them on this occasion. These thugs were obviously street fighters and so Greg decided to match them. As Granit came forward, Greg launched himself into the air and delivered a crushing head butt to Granit's nose, causing it to instantly break and drive bone back into his skull. Granit sank to his knees, unconscious. Ismet was stunned but recovered quickly, leaping at Greg.

But Greg was faster and kicked him between the legs. As Ismet doubled over, he received a knee to the face. He collapsed to the ground, winded and unable to breath properly. Greg stayed still for a second then turned to Hannah,

"Now might be a good time to get the hell out of Dodge!" he said and took her hand.

Hannah was shocked at what she had just witnessed. People carried on walking past, not wishing to get involved. Bouncers on the door of a bar nearby stood stunned. They wouldn't get involved either, not after witnessing that!

"Come on" Greg said calmly, "Grab what you need and leave the rest behind."

She recovered her composure quickly, grabbed her two carrier bags and her favourite jumper and stood next to him. The men still lay on the ground, one unconscious, the other in shock and unable to breath.

"Oh my God!" Hannah exclaimed, "What have you done?"

"They'll be ok soon, too soon, so let's get moving. This way." And he set off towards the railway station. They hustled along quickly and turned left towards the car park. Hannah suddenly held back,

"Where are we going?" she asked.

"Away from here. I have a car in this car park. We need to put some distance between us and those thugs."

"How do I know I can trust you?" she spoke with a tremble.

Greg stopped and looked her in the eye.

"You don't. I'll have to earn that trust, if you'll let me? Your choice, those thugs or me."

She looked back at him. He seemed genuine, and honest too. But she was still unsure.

"Ok," she finally replied. "But don't try anything, ok?"

Greg smiled,

"I wouldn't dream of it. I'm here to help you, nothing else. Shall we go?"

He turned away and set off towards a sports car. It was an MG TF Convertible. In silver with a black soft top roof. It was gleaming, as if straight off the showroom floor. Hannah looked in approval.

"Well, that's a good start" she chuckled.

Greg smiled. His car always drew appreciative looks. Not surprising the money he had lavished on her.

When he was about twenty feet away, he stopped and held her back.

"Wait" he ordered and pressed a button on the key fob. The car lights and indicators lit up and flashed. He waited a few seconds before moving towards the car. He opened the boot and told Hannah to put her bags inside.

"Not much room in the car I'm afraid" he said. She did as he said and stood still.

Greg walked around to the passenger side and held the door open for her.

Somewhat reluctantly she sat inside. Greg then joined her and started the engine. There was a throaty rumble and he took off.

"Seatbelt please" he said and she did as he said. He smiled,

"Safety first."

Hannah was still in shock but found herself relaxing.

Greg turned out of the car park and headed for Princess Road and the way out of Manchester. As he drove, two police cars and an ambulance passed him in the opposite direction.

"See?" Greg said, "They'll be okay soon. Sorry you had to see that."

Hannah stared at him. One minute a fighting machine, the next the perfect gentleman.

'What am I doing here?' she thought.

Chapter 2.

Going Home.

Dardan stood at the foot of the hospital bed, his face a mask of thunder.

"Tell me what happened!" he demanded.

Granit told him truthfully, one did not lie to Dardan and live to tell the tale.

Dardan nodded thoughtfully, recognising the truth. He turned to the Asian doctor who stood, trembling by the side of the bed.

"He can leave now?

The doctor studied Granit, his face a mash of bandages.

"If he so desires." He replied. "There would appear to be no brain damage but I suggest he takes things easy for a few weeks."

Dardan laughed.

"To have the brain damage, one must first have the brain!" he said.

The doctor shrugged.

"I'll give him some pain killers" he muttered.

"No tablets!" Dardan shouted. "He must feel his pain for being a fool!"

Again the doctor shrugged.

"In that case he is free to go. We need the bed."

With that he walked away, glad to be out of this. He knew who these men were and had no intention of getting involved.

Dardan looked at his two men.

"So be it" he said. "This man who beat you up", the two men looked away in embarrassment, "He steals one of my girls. A Crusader perhaps? I will speak to McReanor. He will find out who and where this Crusader is and you, YOU TWO, will retrieve her and deal with this man. Am I understood?"

They both nodded and Granit tried to get off the bed. Ismet helped him and he stood unsteadily.

"Boss, we will find him and I will tear him limb from limb!" Granit said forcefully.

Dardan chuckled,

"Unless he catches you by surprise again, eh?"

With that, the three men left the hospital. Dardan had a call to his pet police officer to make and the other two needed a change of clothes.

Greg steered the sports car skilfully along the M602 until he reached the M62 which headed West. The atmosphere had been tense, Greg constantly checking to make sure they were not followed. Once on the M62 he relaxed slightly and pressed the call button on the car radio.

"Call Harry" he said. There was a brief moment of silence then the sound of a call tone. A few seconds the call was answered.

"Greg old son! What have you been up to?" a gravelly South London voice replied.

"Now Harry, what on earth makes you ask that?"

"The news old son. Seems a couple of heavies belonging to a local gangster had their faces rearranged tonight. I won't ask if you are ok, 'cos I know the answer."

"Long story mate. Do me a favour, keep an ear out on GMP radio net for me? See if they have any clues. I'd appreciate a heads up if they are on my trail."

"Consider it done old son. Now then, apparently there was a girl involved. I take it she's with you right now?"

"Yes Harry. I think she's wondering what the hell she's got into."

Hannah nodded fiercely.

"Well young lady" said Harry, "You need not worry. Greg is the nicest guy you could wish to meet, despite what you may have witnessed this evening. He'll look after you, trust me."

Hannah looked at the radio, as if searching for the person behind the voice.

"Thank you erm, Harry. I kind of have no choice right now do I?"

Harry chuckled,

"Just don't let him play his music in the car! You'll want to go back to Mancunia if he does!!"

Greg smiled,

"You, Harry, are a musical Philistine. Classical Reflection sing like angels. Catch you later old son."

With that Greg disconnected the call. Hannah was looking at him with a quizzical look.

"Sorry, who?"

"Classical Reflection. Twins who sing beautifully. An acquired taste I guess."

Hannah asked "Who is Harry?"

"Harry? He's an old friend. We served together."

"Served? As in, in the army?"

"Yes. Harry lasted longer than I did."

"Why?" Hannah asked curiously.

"Tell you what, let's save that story for later. It's a long one and probably best if Harry tells it. It sounds more sort of romantic the way he tells it."

As they drove along, the atmosphere got slightly better. Hannah asked questions about Greg's work and he answered truthfully. She then asked where exactly they were going.

"Snowdonia" Greg told her. "I have a cottage near a small village. It's on its own land, about fifty acres and is quite secluded."

Hannah looked worried.

Greg spoke to calm her fears.

"Look, please don't worry. I've lived there about ten years. It's isolated because my work demands it. It is secure and no one will get near without me knowing. Oh, and there's Sav."

"Sav? Who is Sav?"

"More of a what really. Sav is an ex-Army War Dog. He's nine years old and was retired due to his age. He's still got what it takes and, trust me, will protect you and me with his life if necessary. When we get there, stay in the car and I'll explain the situation to him."

Hannah looked at him aghast.

"Sorry, but you will explain the situation to a DOG?"

Greg chuckled.

"He's more than a dog. He's trained to kill at the word of

command but, if you or I were in danger, he'd kill to protect us. I just need to tell him you are a friend and he'll understand."

Hannah did not seem convinced though.

Greg had forgotten that the CD player in his car sometimes had a mind of its own. As he concentrated on the road ahead, music filled the car.

'Shotgun', sung by George Ezra played and they listened until,

"Time flies by in the yellow and green" played and Hannah started to join in. She had a lovely voice for one so young. When the chorus played, Greg joined in too.

"I'll be riding shotgun, underneath the hot sun,

Feeling like a someone" they both sang.

Hannah looked across and chuckled. Pretty soon they were both singing at the tops of their voices and giggling like children.

When the track ended, they roared with laughter and fist bumped.

"Oh my!" said Hannah, "I haven't laughed that much in years. And you're not so bad, well, for an old guy!"

Greg laughed again.

"Not so much of the old eh?" he chuckled.

They played the track again and loved every second of the companionship it brought. Hannah looked across at Greg.

"Thanks" she said, simply.

Greg just nodded, not sure how to answer. He was feeling strange.

'Maybe it's the adrenalin slowing down' he thought.

He saw that Hannah had relaxed and, with her head against the window, had closed her eyes. After a few minutes it was obvious she was fast asleep.

'Good. Best cure for the shock she's had.'

He made sure the radio would not disturb her if it rang and settled in to the one and a half hours driving he had ahead of him. His mind was full of questions and very few answers.

Where do we go from here?

What do I do about this bloody Mafia mob?

How do I look after this girl?

What the hell will Conner say?

As the journey progressed he made a plan, of sorts. He would take the fight to the Mafia only if they troubled him or Hannah. Right now she needed him. For protection, for security and for a decent future. Money was no object to Greg but he had to be careful it didn't look like charity to Hannah. That would be tricky. Then she needed clothes, those she had on would need burning. She needed to clean up. Tact and diplomacy would be vital here.

Just then Greg had an idea. Tracey!

Tracey was a local lady who ran the local pub. Greg could trust her for advice of a female kind. Greg had not been involved with a female for over ten years. To say he was out of practice was a gross understatement. His house was decorated in a masculine way mostly, although Tracey had helped with advice on colours in most rooms. With one exception, the lounge. That was Greg's domain and he cherished it. Conner said it was like stepping back in time. 'Old world sort of' he said. Good job he hadn't seen the cellar! It was like a military armoury.

Greg concentrated on the road whilst keeping an eye out behind. He saw nothing to concern him and relaxed, eager to get home and show Hannah just how secure her life would be.

Chapter3.

Davey

Sergeant Davey McReanor had been a police officer for twenty years. The fact that he'd only reached Sergeant was down to his arrogant attitude to his superiors. He was disdainful of Graduate Entries, Senior Officers who hadn't set foot on a street before reaching the rank of Inspector and above.

At six feet three and weighing in at eighteen stone, Davey was feared by most of his colleagues as a vicious bully. Criminals didn't make complaints against him for fear of their lives. His colleagues let Davey into any brawls first, mostly in the hope that someone would, one day, kick the shit out of him! With his Zappata moustache, he thought he looked like Omar Sharif. Sadly he didn't but many females found him attractive, especially young impressionable probationers. They didn't date him twice though. Davey liked rough sex. Most females didn't, so Davey used the girls on the streets, without paying, of course. That was how Dardan had discovered him. McReanor had beaten a prostitute very badly and she belonged to Dardan. The Mafia boss was furious and arranged to have McReanor brought to him.

By the time Davey arrived, he was covered in blood and had several broken ribs. He had screamed at Dardan that he was police and should be shown some damn respect.

With that Dardan had slapped him hard across the face and kicked him in the crutch.

"RESPECT?" Dardan had screamed. "You fucking bastard polis! You beat up one of MY girls and demand respect?

McReanor lay quiet, knowing when he was beaten.

Dardan had outlined what he wanted from his pet polis from now on and Davey had no choice but to accept. He would have money paid into his bank account, despite his refusal. Dardan was clever. Once the first payment went in, McReanor was HIS!

McReanor was cleaned up and driven home, from where he called in sick for five days. If anyone noticed his slight limp, they didn't mention it.

From then on, if any of Dardans' businesses were to be targeted, Davey would tip them off. A payment would arrive shortly after. Davey also gave them information on the competition and would actively target them to give Dardan more business. Drugs, guns, prostitutes, all fell into the mafia bosses lap, courtesy of Sgt Davey McReanor.

As he strolled along the street in Manchester City Centre, he felt his mobile phone buzz. The ringtone was switched off as he was on duty. He stopped, looked around and stepped into a shop doorway.

Looking at the screen he saw it was Dardan Flaka. He sighed. Davey knew what the man wanted. He'd heard about the two thugs getting a kicking and secretly admired whoever did it. There couldn't be many in this world who could take down Granit and Ismet Bektashi. As Davey told his colleagues,

"Fuck I'd like to have seen that!"

Especially as it were the twins who had given Davey the kicking he'd so richly deserved.

He pressed answer and waited.

"Speak fuzz!" growled Dardan.

"I'm on the street, on duty. What do you want?"

Dardan sighed. Maybe this polis needed another lesson in respect?

"You heard what happened to the twins?"

"I did." A non-committal response was needed here.

"Find out who did this. CCTV, witnesses, anything. Then I want this bastard's name and address. You have one hour, or the twins will be asking for the information. Comprende?"

Davey understood alright and a shiver ran down his spine.

'Time for a transfer maybe?' he thought.

"I'll do my best" he replied.

"NO! Do better. One hour. The clock, she is ticking!"

Davey made sure the call was disconnected before muttering "Albanian bastard! One day pal, one fine fucking day!"

Chapter 4.

Settling in.

The M62 ran straight onto the A55 for North Wales. Greg carried on, almost driving like an automaton. Eventually he took the turn for Bangor and approached the roundabout. Taking a left he headed for Caernarfon. Hannah stirred and looked at him.

"Where are we?" she asked, sleepily.

"Nearly home" Greg replied, smiling. "How are you feeling?"

"Sorry, I went to sleep." She said, yawning. "I guess I was tired."

"No need to apologise" Greg said, "You must have needed it. Be home in about fifteen minutes."

Hannah gazed through the window at the mountains, light cloud decorating the peaks.

"Is that Snowdon?" she asked.

"Snowdonia, but not the mountain of Snowdon. You can see the peak of Snowdon from our house. On a good day you can see the steam from the trains as they go up."

Hannah noted the use of the word 'our' when he mentioned the house. Was this a good omen? Time will tell, she thought.

After a few more minutes, Greg slowed and turned onto a road through a village. Then, having passed many picturesque houses, he took a track which seemed to lead up into the mountain. Hannah tensed. This was alien to her and she was scared.

Greg took note and smiled. "We have a pub and a good shop. There's even a garage to help fix my cars when they break down."

"Cars?" Hannah asked. "More than one?"

Greg congratulated himself. His diversion tactic had worked.

"Yes. When we get snow a 4x4 is vital. Or you could ski. Or, as I do, you fall over when skiing!"

Hannah laughed as the vision of Greg on his backside skiing filled her mind. She watched as they drove along the track before stopping just short of a large wrought iron gate. Written on a chunky piece of Welsh slate was one word. 'Llamedos'

Hannah asked what the name meant. Greg merely said, "read it backwards!"

Hannah did so and burst out laughing.

"Sod em all! Brilliant!"

Greg took a remote control from the glove compartment and pressed it. The gate slid to the right and, when it was wide enough, Greg drove through.

Hannah was astounded. Not just by the gate but the vista beyond. As far as the eye could see were fields. Many held sheep but two had horses watching them. In the distance, at the top of a rise, was a large stone-built cottage. She could see a long conservatory as the late evening sun glinted off the windows.

"Wow" she whispered, "Is that all yours?"

"Ours from now on Hannah" Greg replied. "It's your home for as long as you want it. Any time you want to leave, please, just say so. Is that a deal?"

She looked across at him.

"Are you for real? I mean, do you mean that? Honest?"

"Honest. Give it some time though. Let's get those Albanians off our backs first. I might need Harry's help with that. He's a computer whizz."

Hannah returned her attention to the house that was fast approaching. Single storey, long and deep, it looked quite shabby. But, 'hey,' she thought, ironically, 'beggars can't be choosers.'

Greg slowed and parked away from the main door, a solid mahogany thing which looked, to Hannah's eyes, impregnable. A large triple garage sat off to the left, again stone-built with a

Welsh slate sloping roof.

Greg looked at her.

"Please, wait here for a minute. I need to talk to Sav."

He stepped out of the car and went to the door.

"Sav!" he called, "It's me!"

Opening the door, which appeared not to have been locked, he stood aside. A huge German Shepherd dog bounded out and jumped up, barking and licking Greg's face. Greg fussed him then spoke one word.

"Down." The dog sat immediately. Greg squatted and whispered dramatically in the dogs' ears, looking across to the car where Hannah sat trembling. The dog also looked across and, strangely, seemed to be listening.

Greg stood and walked back to the car, Sav following, ears back and alert. He opened Hannah's door and told Sav to sit. He did so.

"It's ok to get out now, but just stand still and let him sniff you."

Hannah slowly, very slowly exited the car. Sav looked her up and down and then looked at Greg, almost asking permission to approach this stranger.

Greg instead took Hannah's hand and held it out to Sav.

"Sav, this is Hannah. Friend. Okay?"

The dog gazed at them both, seemingly confused.

"Friend" Greg said again.

Sav approached the girl and sniffed her.

"Oh my God!" Hannah exclaimed, "I must stink! I'm so sorry Sav!"

At hearing his name spoken by this girl, Sav stopped and looked up. He then did the strangest thing as far as Greg was concerned.

He lay down and then rolled onto his back. Greg was astonished. Sav had never done this before. Hannah, however, recognised what he wanted and squatted down and rubbed Sav's tummy. The dog revelled in the attention.

"Well I'm buggered!" Greg said smiling. "That's a first I must say. I reckon you've got a friend there Hannah."

Hannah was thrilled. After a few minutes Greg led the two indoors. Sounding rather like a trainee estate agent, he gave the guided tour.

"First left, a single bedroom. First right, bathroom. Second right kitchen, second and third left, double bedrooms, choose which you want later. Third right is the lounge and straight ahead the conservatory. The glass is special. Bullet proof and no one can see in from the outside, even with the lights on. We can see out though. Saves buying curtains!" he added, embarrassed that he'd spoken for too long.

Hannah stood and tried to take it all in. After six years on the streets she was in danger of being overwhelmed, a fact Greg recognised.

"Fancy a brew?" he said.

Hannah looked at him.

"Can I make it? She asked shyly.

"Wow, someone making me a cup of coffee? I could get *used* to this!" he said, causing them both to collapse with laughter, remembering a line from 'Shotgun'.

He showed her where the kettle and other things were in the kitchen and left to collect her belongings from the car, before parking it in the garage. Hannah could see him from the kitchen window and watched carefully. This was crazy, she thought. In a minute I'll wake up and discover I'm back on the street. While the kettle boiled, she opened cupboards and, again, was astounded. One cupboard held tins and jars of every food she could imagine. Another held packet foods and UHT milk. You could live for a year on this alone, she thought. When she opened the fridge, again there was an ample supply of food, cheeses, cold meats, butters. The freezer next to the fridge was crammed with foods, meats, pies, chips and so on. In yet another cupboard were dozens of tins of dog food, along with bags of dog biscuits. Just then Greg came into the room.

"I like to be prepared" he said. Hannah just nodded.

"Err, I've left your bags in the hall, just until you choose your bedroom."

"Thanks" was all she could manage, starting to feel embarrassed at her appearance.

"Right, milk and two sugars for me please. Mugs are…"

"I saw them, they're beautiful" Hannah said.

"Local artist sells them." Greg replied. "I'll be in the conservatory."

With that, Greg turned and walked away, his mind full of thoughts.

After making the coffee, Hannah took them towards the conservatory. Stepping inside she stopped abruptly. The room was about twenty feet deep and fifty feet wide with floor to ceiling windows all along the front. The view was simply stunning. In the distance she could actually see the summit of Snowdon, something she'd only seen on tv programmes before. The house was high on a hill and the view stretched for miles.

"Wow what a view!" she said.

Greg, who had been sat to one side, stood and took one of the mugs of coffee.

"Yes, I never get tired of it. Especially in the winter. Have a seat." He pointed to one of three large leather settees. It was then that Hannah took in the room. As well as the settees, there were two coffee tables, a dining table and ten chairs, and, in one corner, a massive computer station. Pictures of views of Wales were scattered around the walls. The pride of place, however, was a painting. It showed a Union Jack, and, underneath, were two soldiers, painted in silhouette, arm in arm, walking a path of poppies. She could see that the poppies were painted using fingerprints. Three military emblems adorned the lower part of the painting. She stood gazing at it, carefully sipping her coffee. The white, yes she thought, white, plush carpet felt deep beneath her feet and she immediately took off her scruffy trainers.

Greg moved beside her.

"It's called Path of Peace" he said quietly. "Painted for me by Kirsty Chapman."

"Is she famous" Hannah asked, feeling stupid.

"Not yet, but one day" Greg replied.

"I love it" Hannah said, in awe.

"There's more in the lounge" Greg said and led the way.

The lounge was also huge. One long window filled the far wall and the others had many photos and pictures. The walls were painted a deep red which set off the pictures perfectly. Hannah moved around the room slowly, taking in each and every picture. She stopped at a photo of a young man, longish hair, smiling at the camera.

"Your son?" she asked.

"Yes, Conner. He's 19 now."

Hannah moved on then stopped abruptly at a large framed print. The background was dark green. In the middle was what looked to her like a military badge. Surrounding the badge were passport type photos of men and women, all in a uniform. There were, according to the writing at the bottom, 300 'Murdered colleagues.' Her eyes stopped at one photo and she caught her breath. Hannah read the name and date beneath the photo and studied the face intensely. It showed a pretty woman, round face, short dark hair. She had an almost Pixie look to her. Then it dawned on her. Turning to Greg she said, coldly,

"I'm not her!"

Greg looked at her.

"I know. I couldn't help her. If you let me, I can help you." With that he left the room and went back to the conservatory. Hannah breathed out. She felt bad at her comment. Looking down, she noticed that Sav was lying at her side, gazing up at her.

Kneeling beside the dog she said "I'm sorry Sav. I shouldn't have said that. Do you think he'll forgive me?" Sav licked her hand gently then lay with his head on his huge paws.

"Yes, you're right Sav. I'll apologise to him now."

She walked into the conservatory, noting that the light outside was fading but inside remained bright. Sav followed behind. Greg was sat at the computer station, tapping his fingers over the keyboard quickly. Sav sat between them.

Before Hannah could speak, Greg said,

"Pull up a chair next to me. It's occurred to me that you might want clothes?"

Hannah grabbed a rolling computer chair, again in plush leather, and sat beside him. She felt, rather than saw, Sav lie over her feet. Somehow it felt right, homely.

Greg keyed the internet and said,

"Right, let's see what we can get delivered tomorrow. Then off to Chester shopping next week. Caernarfon and Bangor are like ghost towns when it comes to shops."

For the next hour they pored over various websites and Greg ordered her a selection of jeans, dresses, skirts and blouses in all sorts of colours and patterns. He also ordered her a selection of trainers, once she'd told him she was a size 4. He had guessed correctly that she was a size eight to ten in clothes. Eventually they sat back.

"Are you hungry?" he asked.

"Starving!" Hannah responded, "But first, I'm sorry for my comment. It must seem ungrateful."

Greg smiled somewhat sadly.

"That's okay" he said. "Let's forget it eh?"

Hannah agreed readily. She was relieved that he didn't hold

a grudge. Just then a buzzer sounded.

"Fuck sake!" Greg muttered, "That'll be Harry. Mention food and his bloody antenna goes into overdrive!" he chuckled.

He changed the screen on the computer and, sure enough, Harry was parked by the gate, sounding his horn and waving manically. Greg pressed a key and they watched as the gate slid open. Once Harry had driven through, Greg closed the gate. Within minutes there was a knock at the door and Sav bounded towards it, barking and growling.

"Down!" Greg called. Speaking to Hannah he said,

"Even Harry gets the treatment from Sav. He loves him but unless he sees him, he remains on alert."

He walked to the door and opened it. Harry peered inside,

"Is that bloody death dog in there?" he called. Sav, hearing this bounded forward and jumped up, licking Harry.

"As per usual Harry, you are just in time for dinner!" Greg said.

"I hope it's a bloody take away and not your cooking!" Harry responded, winking at Hannah.

Greg made the introductions and offered them both a glass of wine.

Harry smiled at Hannah,

"Wine he calls it. More like anti-freeze!"

They all went into the kitchen. Hannah looked at Greg sadly.

"Look, I'm not that presentable, may I have a bath?"

Greg looked at her and said,

"Of course. There are fresh towels. I'm afraid there's only Head and Shoulders shampoo. We can stock up tomorrow."

Hannah nodded gratefully. She felt overpowered by Harry, him being a larger than life character. Pleasant though.

It was then that a realisation hit Greg.

"Oh hell!" he exclaimed. "I mean, erm, you'll sort of need, well, you know, sort of 'ladies' things! Sorry, I haven't got any."

Hannah and Harry exchanged glances and Harry burst out laughing!

"I never thought I'd see the day, old son, when Greg is embarrassed! Look at the colour he's gone!"

Greg took a playful swipe at his friend.

"Feck off will ye!"

Hannah chuckled,

"I'll cope, don't worry. What's for dinner by the way?"

"Beef Stifado. That's beef in red wine with shallots and spices. Is that ok?"

"Perfect" she said and sashayed out of the room to get her shower.

Harry looked at the door.

"We need to talk mate. You are in a shit load of trouble with some fucking bad people!"

Hannah closed the bathroom door and slid the bolt. She gazed around at the corner glass shower, the pedestal sink and the stand-alone bath. A toilet completed the suite. Everything was in white, from the suite to the glistening tiles on the four walls. To her left was a frosted glass window with an extractor fan above. Next to it was a full-length glass mirror.

She switched on the light and the fan kicked in, causing her to jump.

She laughed at herself. Bath or shower? Hmm, choices for a change, she thought before deciding on a shower. She stepped in and turned the temperature as high as it would go before running the water. Quickly she stepped back out and undressed, suddenly ashamed of the filthy clothes she wore. Once naked she stood before the mirror and gasped. Her slender body was absolutely filthy and she cried in shame for a few minutes.

Eventually she pulled herself together and stepped into the cubicle, wincing at the heat of the water. She sighed,

'It might be bloody hot, but it's bloody beautiful!'

She grabbed the shampoo and washed her hair three times, revelling in the feeling of soft silky hair beneath her fingers. Then she took the scented shower gel and literally scrubbed her whole body until it was red, but clean. There was a nail brush on a corner shelf and she used that on her feet and finger nails, not resting until they were immaculately clean.

Finally, Hannah felt clean and, almost, respectable. It was one hell of a long time since that had happened. She turned off the shower and stepped from the cubicle onto plush carpet. On a heated shower rail were several clean bath towels and she wrapped herself in two of them, feeling the luxurious softness as she sat on the edge of the bath. The steam was evaporating now and so she looked around for something clean to wear. On the back of the door hung a Royal Blue dressing gown, it was polyester and looked and felt brand new. She put it on, it felt glorious against her newly scrubbed skin. A tad long but that was no problem. She belted it up, threw her old clothes in the waste bin and left the room, feeling happier than ever before.

Chapter 5.

Harry.

It took almost the whole hour for McReanor to get the info Dardan wanted. Davey got a probationer onto cctv of the area and, to be fair, she was good. After getting the number plate, she searched the Police National Computer and found the drivers name and address. Printing it off, she took it to the Sergeant and beat a hasty retreat before he could ask her out.

McReanor sat and studied the paper.

"Gotcha ya bastard!" he muttered angrily. Whilst feeling some admiration for this man, he felt pissed off at the aggro it was causing him. The Detectives in charge of the investigation were curious as to why Davey was interested but he managed to fob them off. They weren't that interested in finding the assailant anyway. Their opinion was that the twins had got what they deserved.

McReanor grabbed his phone and sent a text to Dardan with the details. He didn't get a reply, not even a bloody thanks! Davey fumed but was sensible enough to realise there was nothing he could do about things as they stood.

Davey sat at his desk and remembered better days. He had joined the force, as it was called then, aged eighteen. Fresh out of Training College he had been thrust into the station at Moss Side, the toughest beat in Manchester. Partnered with a grizzly old copper, he had learned the faces to watch. Villains steered clear of the two as they patrolled, except for one wide boy who wanted to enhance his reputation by smacking a copper.

Tolly chose the wrong copper though, and ended up in casualty with no teeth left and a bad case of concussion. No action was taken against Constable McReanor.

A few weeks later, three cardboard gangsters attempted to rob a High Street bank. Davey was around the corner and, as the robbers left the building, charged at them, truncheon flailing, laying the three out cold. Again, no action was taken against him. After finishing his two years' probation, McReanor started getting cocky and was rapidly taken down a peg or two by his Sergeant, a bull of a man with a fist the size of a ham!

McReanor quietened down until the Sergeant retired. On the night of the retirement party, as the outgoing officer staggered home, he was attacked from behind and severely beaten. Most people suspected McReanor but no proof was ever found.

Over the years McReanor was commended for bravery several times but promotion eluded him. He passed his Sergeants exam with flying colours but no vacancies were offered to him. Until one night, whilst on mobile patrol, McReanor saw a BMW being driven erratically. Being observant, Davey knew the car belonged to his Superintendent and pulled it over. The Super blew over the limit and knew his career was over. Until Davey called a taxi company and sent him home. The situation was never mentioned again but, three weeks later, Sergeant Davey McReanor was transferred to Central in Manchester. Since then fortune had not favoured him in his pursuit of promotion, but he knew it was only a matter of time.

Davey put Dardan and his problems from his mind and set out on patrol. Time to break a few heads, he thought.

While Greg heated up the meal he'd prepared that morning, Harry sat and updated him.

"Some Sergeant in Central has tracked you down. He's a paid cop for Dardan Flaka, an Albanian gangster. He's one mean bastard mate. You've made him lose face and, when you're into every racket going, that is something he cannot, nor will, forgive. With them it's a' till I die' vendetta. Remember 'Taken' with Liam Neeson? Multiply that by ten old son. I was too late to block the PNC check so now they know who you are and where you live. I guess they'll pay you a visit soon mate. I'll stay if you like?"

Greg sat and took a sip of his wine.

"Nah, you're alright. I doubt they'll come tonight. They need to recce first, see how vulnerable I am. And one of his thugs won't be much use to him. Get the Security team together.

I want them here by morning. They know what to do."

They both heard the shower stop and knew that Hannah would soon appear. They sat quietly until she stood in the doorway. Sav sat by her side, like her faithful new friend. Hannah had washed her hair, probably several times and it shone jet black. She had put on a dressing gown that Greg kept behind the bathroom door and was almost unrecognisable as the street urchin Greg had rescued. The two men sat open mouthed.

"So, do I scrub up well?" Hannah said, laughing at their faces. Now it was the turn of both men to be embarrassed.

"Er yes" Greg said, "It's just that I've never seen anyone wearing that dressing gown before."

Hannah stepped forward and sniffed the cooking pot.

"Smells gorgeous" she said, "Is it ready?"

"Sure is" Greg said. "Er, is it okay if we eat off our laps guys?"

Hannah breathed a sigh of relief. The thought of sitting at that magnificent glass table had petrified her. Yet again Greg was on the button.

'It's almost as if he can read my mind' she thought.

Greg put the huge pot of Beef Stifado and a smaller pot of mashed potato on the work top and they helped themselves. Harry obviously taking the larger portion.

Then they went into the conservatory.

Hannah was worried.

"Are you sure no one can see in?" she asked.

Greg beckoned to her and they went out of a side door, onto a large wooden veranda. He pointed at the windows which were totally dark.

"You see, no one can see in."

Hannah breathed another sigh of relief.

"Thanks Greg" she said, for the first time using his name.

The three sat eating, Hannah was fastest and asked for seconds, to which she helped herself. Harry glanced at Greg.

"Look old son, what you are doing is, well, admirable and all. But that is one impressionable young woman. She might sort of get the wrong idea. You know?"

Greg frowned. That thought had occurred to him.

"I'll be careful mate" he replied. "Her safety is priority though."

Harry nodded but kept his thoughts to himself.

Chapter 6.

The Team.

Dardan Flaka sat nursing a large brandy. He reclined in the luxury of the red leather furniture in an alcove in his nightclub. Named. "Albana" after his daughter, the club was sited in Wilmslow. Many professional footballers and celebrities frequented his club, and he made a fortune supplying anything they wanted. And that meant ANYTHING!

The girl, Hannah, was one of those things. Even at the age of 24, she could pass for fourteen and that was a big selling point to Flaka. He had 'clients' queuing to take this girl and they must not be kept waiting any longer. But now some damned "quifsha pidhin" (fucking pussy) had stolen her! Flaka was incandescent with rage and had instructed his chief Lieutenant to meet him at the club.

Known as Dada, the Albanian looked after all of Dardans girls and did a good job. But Hannah had eluded him and so Flaka knew who to send after her.

The lighting was subtle in the club but Flaka made out his daughter, Albana, coming towards him, leading a short swarthy man in a three-piece pin stripe suit.

"Papa, your guest has arrived. Should I get him a drink?"

"He won't be here long enough to drink it!" Flaka snapped, glaring at his second in command.

"Sit!" he ordered.

Dada sat.

"The girl, Hannah, has been taken from me Dada. You will recover her. Quickly! Here is the thief's name and address. How you do it is no concern of mine. But this Angel must be made to pay for his insult to me. Do it and send me the video. Now go."

Dada knew when to keep quiet and left quickly. Once in his chauffer driven BMW X5, he called his top man.

He told Luan what to do and how to do it. Four men should be enough. Straight to this house in Wales, charge in, kill Angel, collect the girl and gone. Just like that.

Luan agreed to set off the next morning and be in Wales by nine am.

Dada hung up and sat back.

"Home" he instructed his driver. "Easy money!"

Greg, Hannah and Harry sat in the conservatory, glasses of wine in hand. Greg outlined his plan.

"Harry, I want the full perimeter security team here by dawn. All ten of them. Four on the front gate, armed, two of those visible, two non-visible. I predict they'll come tomorrow; mob handed. Who have we got available from the in-house security team?"

Harry consulted his laptop.

"Good news, we've got Legs Diamond, Sepp and Jack, Pilgrim and Tiny Tim, all coming here tonight, together. They've been on standby since I called them earlier. I had a feeling you'd want them asap."

Greg smiled, "Six in house. Excellent. When they come we'll get them in the barn straight away. Get them settled then disperse them around the estate with the perimeter mob."

Harry nodded.

"In that case I'll wait at the gatehouse for them and sort them out. I'll leave you two alone. Get some sleep Greg, I have a feeling that tomorrow is going to be a busy day!"

Harry let himself out, Sav totally ignored him, concentrating on Hannah rubbing his ears.

"Greg" she said, "Some of those names. Tiny Tim? Is he short? Does Legs actually have legs?" she chuckled.

Greg smiled at her.

"I'll let them do the introductions in the morning." He said, winking.

"It'll be an eye opener!"

Then he broached the subject of the sleeping arrangements.

"look, if you want to choose your bedroom?"

Hannah hesitated, suspecting something more was coming.

"Well, I guess the spare double?"

Greg nodded. "Although I've had an idea…"

Hannah raised her eyebrows,

"Don't panic" Greg added hurriedly, "It's just that I suggest you do take that bedroom and use the single room next door as a sort of walk in wardrobe? I mean, with twenty-six parcels being delivered tomorrow, I doubt you'll want them all in your bedroom? I hope that makes sense?"

Hannah visibly relaxed.

"Thanks, that's a great idea. You had me worried for a minute."

"I noticed," he replied. "Look, worrying you is not something that I will ever do intentionally. As far as I'm concerned, you're family now. "

Hannah looked at the carpet, tears filling her eyes.

'Family.' A word she had not used or heard for years.

"I don't know how to thank you" she said quietly. Sav looked up at her and placed his head on her lap.

"You can thank me by being happy. That'll do for me" Greg said and meant every word.

On his computer, Greg saw Harry approach the gatehouse carefully. It was safe but always check, Greg thought. Nothing was untoward and Harry entered. No lights came on. The building was set back from the gate which is why Hannah had not seen it when they arrived. It was also well camouflaged; it couldn't be seen at night. In the gate house were gate controls, light switches and a communications system, both to the house and the police. Sited some fifty yards along the lane to the house, was a hidden surprise. Should any vehicle manage to break through the gates, Harry could trigger a ramp to spring up out to the ground. This would cause the offending vehicle to flip and crash. Checking no one was around, Harry pressed the release button. The ramp slid up smoothly and swiftly. Satisfied, Harry lowered it again. It had never been used in anger but he suspected that time was not far off.

Back in the house, while Greg worked on his computer, Hannah wandered around the conservatory. At the far end, next to a door that led outside, was a walnut bookcase, crammed with books. Hannah took one and read the title out loud, "The Dandelion Clock" A wish to end all wishes, a war to end all wars" she read. Greg moved alongside her.

"It's a great book, a sort of love story about World War One."

Hannah opened it, "It's signed!" she exclaimed. "Do you know the author?"

"I've read all her books" Greg replied. "Why not give it a go yourself?"

"I will" she said and moved towards a sofa. Harry took a remote control and pressed play for the CD player. Gradually, music filtered through the surround sound speakers and the angelic voices of Classical Reflection filled the room. Hannah looked at Greg. He seemed to be in another world. She had to admit, Harry was wrong. These girls could sing!

"Do you mind if I stay up with you?" she asked, timidly, almost like a child.

"Of course not" Greg said, "In fact, stay up and meet the guys when they arrive. I think they'd like that as well."

Hannah nodded. She was apprehensive but, with Greg there, she knew she'd be safe.

Greg suggested they take their wine onto the decking. The evening was warm and they sat on comfortable wicker chairs, in almost total darkness. The nearest lights were over a mile away and the clear sky showed millions of stars. Hannah gazed up at them.

"It's so beautiful here, and so quiet. I think I'm going to like it here. But I want to earn my keep. Would you let me do things, like cooking and stuff?" she asked Greg.

He thought about it for a moment. He wanted Hannah to have a rest and build her strength up. On top of that, he had plans to involve her in his business but guessed that doing some cooking wouldn't be a problem."

"Ok" he replied, "Being cooked for? I could get *used* to this!"

They both chuckled quietly, Sav sitting between them, happily looking around. At about a quarter to twelve, Sav sat bolt upright and looked towards the gate. Lights appeared on the road to the house and Greg saw Harry leave the gatehouse and slip into the undergrowth. Greg grabbed Hannah and ushered her inside.

"Stay here!" he said, "It's probably Legs and co but I'm not taking any chances. Harry's got the gate covered."

He went back outside and squatted by the decking posts. As if from nowhere, a pistol appeared in his hand and he waited patiently. Soon a minibus turned towards the gate and a horn sounded. A voice called loudly,

"Fucking open up 'Arry, I need a piss!"

Greg chuckled. Legs would never change. Harry appeared by the passenger door and banged on the window,

"Ladies present you peasant!" and opened the gate. With a shower of loose gravel, the minibus took off up the track, screeching to a halt outside the barn conversion and Legs raced inside. Hannah came onto the decking and noticed the pistol.

"You won't shoot much with that from here" she giggled, "I didn't know James Bond was here!"

Greg looked at her in amazement.

"It's a Walther PPK yes, and okay for close up work. How the hell do you know about them?"

"I've watched all the Bond films Greg," she replied, amused at his expression.

Greg relaxed and felt silly. Of course she would have. She's not been locked up all her life!

A few minutes later the front door opened and five men entered. Sav raced towards them enthusiastically. Hannah, feeling self-conscious wearing just a dressing gown, stayed in the background. Greg strode forward, shaking their hands.

"Welcome gentlemen, let me introduce you to Hannah. Hannah, I give you Legs, Sepp, Jack, Tim and Pilgrem"

Hannah shyly shook their hands. Each man was different. Legs was tall, rangy, with a shock of ginger hair and an untidy ginger moustache. He wore old jeans and a Meatloaf t shirt. Sepp was blonde, tall and handsome. He wore new jeans and a white button-down shirt. He bowed when they shook hands. Jack was short and squat. His round face bore a continual smile. Tim was massive! At least six feet six inches, he towered over Hannah and she had to look almost to the ceiling to see him. Tim wore a blue two-piece suit and a blue, open neck shirt. Pilgrem was different. He was about the same height as Greg but like a barrel. No fat, just muscle. Hannah looked at him curiously.

"Pilgrem? Is that your nickname?"

Pilgrem answered in a deep fake American voice.

"It surely is ma'am. It's because I love John Wayne films."

Hannah lowered her eyebrows and said,

"The hell you do!"

The whole team roared with laughter and Legs proclaimed,

"Hannah, you have just been adopted as our sister! Welcome to the crew."

At that, Harry walked in.

"The perimeter team have arrived while you lot were relaxing. I've set them to work. Now then, any chance of a brew?"

Hannah made to move towards the kitchen but Tiny Tim stopped her.

"It's ok Hannah" he said in a deep West Country voice, "But we make it a point to show new members of our team some hospitality and nominate Legs to get the kettle on."

Legs scowled at him but complied.

As the team took seats, Greg stood in the middle.

"Right then. Let me introduce you to this bunch of reprobates properly" he chuckled.

Tiny Tim sighed dramatically,

"Oh shit, he's going to make a speech!"

Hannah chuckled, the banter between these men was incredible.

Greg spoke loudly, so that Legs could hear in the kitchen,

"If I may be allowed to continue? Thank you. Now then, Legs the tea boy is actually our explosives expert."

Hannah gasped, "Explosives? What for?"

Tiny Tim put his massive hand on hers,

"Blowing things up my dear" he said gently, "But don't worry, we keeps an eye on him see. We doesn't let him out on his own."

Hannah smiled, realising that Tim was simply putting her at ease.

Greg continued.

"He's also not a bad shot. Anyway, next we have Tiny Tim, who is named for obvious reasons. Tim is our muscle man. I've never seen anyone beat him in a fight and no, Hannah, I haven't tried!"

She looked at both, wondering who would win. It would be close, she guessed.

"Sepp is German but we still love him" said Greg and Sepp bowed. "Sepp is our go to man for sniping. He's easily the best shot I've ever seen. Jack, well Jack here is our token American. There is nothing he doesn't know about vehicles and can steal anything we want, convert it and hide it. MI5 would never find it. He's ex United States Marine but apart from that he's ok."

Jack smiled at Hannah and it was an enigmatic smile. She liked him.

"You've met Harry. He's our computer whizz kid. Hacking comes naturally to him. On top of all that, every man here is a fully qualified Combat Medic. We have full medical facilities in the barn, and, underneath us is our armoury. Don't panic but there's more explosives beneath your feet than Guy Fawkes had. And it's even more deadly."

Greg saw a worried look on Hannah's face.

"Is it legal?" she asked carefully.

Greg gave his answer some thought. He decided to be honest.

"Not legal in the lawful sense of the word" he said. "But we have authority to possess and use anything we need in the execution of our duties. We are a government accredited Security Advisor and they give us certain leeway. "

Hannah nodded.

"Thank you. This is all a bit too much for me. Do you mind

if I go to bed?"

They stood as one and Hannah said goodnight. Sav walked beside her and went into her bedroom too.

Tim looked at Greg.

"That bloody dog is in love!" he said and the team laughed.

"I think you may be right" Greg said.

Just then Legs brought a tray of teas and coffees in and placed it on the dining room table. They all sat around and exchanged jokes and stories. The atmosphere was electric. Action was coming and they were buoyed up for it.

Chapter 7.

Planning for war.

Hannah slipped under the luxurious duvet, still in her dressing gown. Her mind was in turmoil. Just twelve hours ago, she was homeless and penniless. Then along came a man who had the capacity to beat two thugs up, yet be so kind and tender to her. He was involved in government security and had a team of, it appeared, mercenaries. Yet she felt at home here. This was like an adventure she might see in Hollywood films. She lay back but sleep eluded her. Excitement filled her and she felt something else. She couldn't put her finger on it. Sav lay by her bed, one eye open.

'If this is a dream' she thought, 'it's a beautiful dream.' Sleep still eluded her and so she got out of bed and went back into the conservatory to hear the plans being made.

As Hannah entered the room, the team looked up.

"Come and join us" Greg said. Hannah sat at the table, between Tiny Tim and Sepp.

"We're having a council of war" Jack said, softly.

"I'm so sorry to have got you all involved in this" she said sadly.

Tim put his huge muscular arm gently around the girl.

"Now listen to me my dear" he said, "We're glad to be involved. That Albanian needs taking down, so don't you worry, okay?"

Greg felt a strange tinge of jealousy when he saw Tim's arm around Hannah but shrugged it off quickly.

"I'm not worried now. You're all my family." Hannah replied, looking around the table.

"Does that make Greg the Daddy?" Legs quipped. He stopped smiling when he saw the look on Greg's face. It disappeared as quickly as it came but it disconcerted Legs and he looked away.

Hannah noticed the change in the atmosphere and retorted,

"Well, you are all my brothers now," and smiling cheekily at Greg continued "Even if Greg is the older brother!"

Greg smiled back and said,

"Less of the old!" The icy atmosphere had melted and so Hannah said,

"Well, if you are going to war for me, it's only fair that you should know why."

With that, she poured herself a coffee and started talking.

Chapter 8.

Hannah's story.

Hannah took a deep breath.

"I was born twenty-four years ago in Chester. My Mum wasn't married. I've never known my Father, who he is or where he is. Nothing. Not that I care. Mum was a great mother at first. She had a job, working as a chef in a posh restaurant. I was looked after by various friends until I went to nursery. Then on to school. That's when it all changed.

Mum had a relationship with this fella, an ex-soldier. He was violent towards us both. I was only nine the first time he hit me. Mum went berserk and threw him out. It broke her. She had loved him so much and did everything she could for him. She turned to vodka and then drugs.

Her dealer was also a pimp and whored her out. I stayed away from home as much as possible, leaving school at fifteen. I got a job in the kitchen of a decent restaurant. Mum had taught me how to cook from an early age, so I got promoted to Head Chef. Then Mum met Keith.

He took over her pimping by beating the crap out of the other one. He had this idea that he could put me on the streets too. I refused so he beat me too. That's when I left home, aged eighteen. I had nowhere to live, flats were way too expensive. I had work but no home. Eventually my work suffered and I got the sack."

The room was silent. Hannah looked into Greg's eyes and saw something there she had never seen in anyone before. Admiration. Not sympathy, or hate or fear, but admiration. Greg looked back at her and smiled encouragingly.

"How did you get involved with the Albanian?" he asked gently.

"Granit, the one whose nose you broke, approached me when I was begging one day. He told me I could earn a fortune, pretending to be only fourteen years old. As a prostitute."

Hannah shuddered.

"I felt sick and told him to fuck off. He slapped me and I ran. I'm small and fast. I hid for weeks and didn't see him. Then his twin brother asked me for sex. I told him to fuck off as well! I ran again and kept moving. Chester, Ellesmere Port, Liverpool, then Manchester. I didn't know that bastard had places there or I'd have gone further south. I lasted six years. Oh yes, the so-called authorities offered me places, mostly amongst prostitutes or smack heads."

"Let me guess" said Sepp softly, "You told them to fuck off too?"

Hannah looked at him and smiled sadly.

"You got me!" she said. "Spot on. It was three years ago when Greg first saw me. He was with Conner, his son and, oh God they were so kind! Do you know Greg that, when you walked away, I cried my heart out? You had been so sweet, both of you. I wanted to see you both again but McReanor moved me on. I tried to go back to the shop but he blocked me. I'm sorry."

Greg stood and moved towards her. Tim stood also and gave up his seat. Putting his arms around her Greg whispered,

"You have nothing to be sorry about."

Hannah almost cried but held herself back.

"Then, about three weeks ago, Flaka found me. He gave me an ultimatum. Work for him voluntarily or he would have the twins kidnap me. They would rape me and get me hooked on heroin. That really scared me so I hid. Until you found me Greg. I thought they would kill you; I was so scared."

Greg closed his eyes and clenched his fists. He could feel the old familiar red mist descending and Harry could see it too. He touched Greg's arm gently.

"Time out Boss" he said quietly and stood up. Greg followed suit and the pair went onto the decking.

"Breathe deeply please Greg"

Just then, they heard the clinking of a bottle on a glass. Sepp held out a glass of an amber liquid.

"It's Metaxa Boss" he said.

Greg took it and sniffed carefully.

"Thank you my friend." He murmured, unable to find his full voice. He took a sip and the brandy burned its way down his throat, giving him a warm feeling inside.

"Ok, I'm okay" he said. With that he walked back inside. No one else had moved. Hannah looked at him with curiosity.

"I'm okay Hannah" he said, almost choking on the words. "Thank you for telling us. It makes me at least more determined that this Albanian be made to pay. He must have done this to many other girls. We're going to close down his operation. Starting now. Harry, get onto your contacts. I want to know everywhere this scum has business. Places etc. Every detail. Legs, go into the cellar, check stock. You know what we will need. Sepp, check the weapons with Jack. We won't get much sleep tonight guys, I'm sorry. But it'll be worth it. Okay?"

Every one of them nodded. Next Greg spoke to Tim.

"Check the perimeter team please mate. I want them on the ball. Any problems, get rid. Pilgrem, check the med packs. Then we'll grab some shut eye."

The team split up to carry out their tasks. It would be only an hour before they returned smiling.

"All complete Boss," said Pilgrem. "no issues."

Greg smiled and heaved a sigh of relief.

"Thanks guys. Grab some sleep eh?"

They left him and Hannah sitting at the table. Greg looked at the girl, a look of pure admiration on his face.

'Steady old son' he thought. 'Don't complicate things, focus!'

"I'm going to stay here," he told Hannah. "What would you like to do?"

"I'll stay too, if that's okay?" she replied, her eyes telling him that she did not want to be alone this night. He turned the lights down low and they took a sofa each. He looked across at this waif like woman, who could, quite easily, pass for a fourteen-year-old, and smiled at her.

"It's going to be okay you know" he whispered.

"I know" she whispered back, "I know" and with that, her eyes closed and she fell into a deep sleep.

Chapter 9.

First Blood.

Greg slept fitfully, while Hannah slept soundly. Sav lay on the floor alongside her and seemed not to sleep at all. Shortly before six o'clock, Greg stood up and stretched. He had things to do. He went into the kitchen and switched the kettle on. He also made a pot of filter coffee, knowing that his team would want some. He then put wet and dried food in Sav's bowl and replaced the water. Sav wandered in and Greg fussed him. The dog seemed to have changed in just over twenty-four hours. Not switched allegiance as such, but he'd taken to Hannah in a way Greg had not expected. Greg stepped outside onto the decking. The sun was rising and predicted a warm day. He lit a cigarette, his first for two days.

'Nasty habit' he told himself. But one he enjoyed. He felt her presence, rather than heard her coming and turned to greet her.

"Good morning" she said. "That was some sleep!"

Greg smiled, "Good, hope you feel refreshed."

She nodded, "Can I have a cigarette?"

Greg was surprised.

"I didn't know you were a smoker" he said, offering her the packet.

"Only when I can get some." She replied, accepting a light. The pair stood in companionable silence while they enjoyed their smokes.

Eventually, Greg said,

"There's a supply in the cupboard under the bookcase. Help yourself."

Hannah thanked him but stayed where she was. She didn't feel comfortable doing as she pleased in what she still considered to be Greg's home. Greg looked towards the gate. He could just make out one of the guards, squatting in the bushes, shotgun across his lap. He looked alert and Greg was glad.

"Your parcels should arrive this morning" he said to Hannah, "Of course we all expect a fashion parade!"

Hannah laughed.

"Me a fashion model? Nice thought and thanks for the compliment."

They went back indoors into the kitchen where Hannah poured them a coffee each. Greg picked up a radio and spoke into it.

"Gate."

A voice answered.

"Gate"

"Send two men half a mile along the track towards the village. Tell them to remain out of sight but to warn us if anyone heads our way. Then to follow any visitors to the gate. "

"Roger" came the reply and Greg went back to the conservatory. He watched as two men wearing all black, and also armed with shotguns, detached themselves from bushes opposite the gate and jog away. He was impressed. He hadn't spotted them earlier.

A few minutes later, the team arrived in dribs and drabs. First was Legs and he greeted them warmly, hoping that his faux pas the previous evening was forgiven. Hannah handed him a coffee and returned to the table to read. Then came Pilgrem and Tiny Tim. Hannah greeted Tim warmly and they helped themselves to coffee. Last were Sepp and Jack, both smiling.

"Gutten Morgen" Sepp said. "A lovely day." Hannah smiled.

"Yes, it sure is." Jack nodded at Greg and sat down.

"So Boss, plans for today?"

Greg pondered the question before answering.

"A bit on the hoof really. I want to let the Albanian make the first move then decide a course of action. Harry should be here soon. Hopefully he'll have intel."

Tim asked Hannah about the book she was reading and she spoke enthusiastically about it. Greg was pleased. Rebecca Bryn was a fine writer and he had all of her books in paperback. All signed too.

Five minutes later, the perimeter guard called on the radio.

"House, this is perimeter. Harry on his way in, fast!"

"House Roger, gate, get ready."

Legs, Sepp and Jack grabbed rifles from the rack in the store cupboard while Greg grabbed a Browning Hi Power 9mm pistol. He turned to Hannah,

"Stay here with Tim. I'll be right back"

And as he spoke he was on his way out of the door and racing along the track to the gate. Then he had a thought and spoke into his radio,

"Pilgrem, bring the Merc Sprinter to the gate, we might have need of it." He didn't wait for a response and he knew his order would be obeyed. As he listened he heard Harry's Volvo Estate powering down the lane and signalled the guard to open up. The gate slid back just in time as Harry threw his car through it. The guard closed the gate quickly. Harry climbed out of the Volvo, a sawn-off shotgun in his hand.

"Black Beemer X5 in the village, looked like four up. Asking directions in the shop I think. Maybe five minutes away."

Greg nodded, 'good, at last, some payback' he thought.

Then he directed four perimeter guards to the bushes opposite the gate and he and the rest of the team took cover either side of the gate, behind the solid stone pillars. They didn't have to wait long when the BMW arrived, slowly. It pulled up to the gate and, as the driver was about to press the buzzer, Greg stepped into view. The hand stopped moving and started to retreat into the car when a voice behind him said,

"Keep that fucking hand still!" Two perimeter guards stepped into view on each side of the BMW, rifles at the ready. Then Legs, Harry, Sepp and Jack also showed themselves.

"Get out of the car, hands raised and no sudden moves. Understand?" The driver nodded and opened his door. The three passengers did the same, knowing when they were outgunned. Greg signalled for the gate to be opened and Sepp and Jack stepped forward and expertly searched the four men, coming up with pistols, a couple of knives and a knuckle duster between them. Greg eyed the men. They were all burly but running to fat. The B team then. He made a quick decision,

"Pilgrem" he called, "The Sprinter."

Pilgrem drove down to the gate and stopped. Greg only had to nod at his team members and they leapt on the four thugs, holding them down before tying them up. Gags and hoods followed and they were thrown, quite literally into the Sprinter.

"What now Greg?" Harry asked.

"I think we should return these to sender, don't you?" he chuckled, "But not yet. Bring their car in and park it behind the barn. We'll let them stew for a couple of hours then take them home. Before we go, put them in body bags with a note saying 'alive this time. Don't send them back.' Ok?"

The team nodded and left. Greg walked back to the house and as he walked in, Hannah was looking worried.

"See little one" Tim said to her, "Twas easy. No trouble at all. "Hannah nodded relieved. She wanted to run to hug Greg but stopped herself.

Greg nodded. "We'll let them consider the error of their ways then give them a lift back to Manchester. I'm assuming that Harry here has Flaka's address?" Harry nodded.

"Then we'll return to sender. Right, time for breakfast."

Hannah laughed, "I'm ahead of you. There's a full English on the go, plenty for everyone. Even Tim here!"

Just as they sat down to eat, the gate guard called that a substantial number of parcels had been delivered. Hannah squealed for joy and, forgetting her breakfast, jumped up, excitedly. Greg instructed that the parcels be brought to the house with due haste! The crew carried on eating, except for Harry who had eaten before leaving home.

"I'll help with the parcels Boss" he told Greg. They heard the front door open and box after bag after box being brought in.

Harry called out,

"For fuck sake Greg, what did you order?"

"Just some bare necessities." Greg called back. "I'm taking Hannah shopping to Chester next week for some more."

"Take the Sprinter!" laughed Harry as he put yet more parcels into the single bedroom, "And a second mortgage!"

Breakfast over, and the dishes washed up by Sepp and Legs, the crew sat at the dining table. Harry updated them.

"Right, I've got Flaka's home address in Wilmslow. Posh place. Lives there with Albana, his daughter. Word is that Flaka is a pussy compared to this bitch. Attractive but god help the man who goes near her. Also, I've got the addresses of a warehouse in Birkenhead Flaka uses for his 'import/export' business and other things. He's got drug dealers all over Manchester and thugs that deliver drugs and collect money every Friday evening. That's five teams of two. Same run, same time every week. And yes Greg, I'm ahead of you. I've got surveillance on each pair 24/7. Any change they'll let me know. He also has a night club in Wilmslow, strangely enough called the Albana. His daughter runs it. There's gambling, pole dancing and rooms for his clients to use for whatever purpose. Again I've got a covert team set up nearby."

Greg thanked him. He was just about to speak when a new Hannah walked into the room. She went straight to Greg and hugged him.

"Thank you!" she gushed, "You thought of everything, and I mean everything" she beamed, proudly showing off a brand-new pair of slim jeans and a white blouse. Beneath could be seen a black bra. Greg smiled back.

"My pleasure. Now then, I know a hairdresser who does house calls. Shall I give her a call and see if she's free today?"

Hannah jumped up and down, "Please!" she cried, "That would be ace!"

Five minutes later Greg told her that Tracey, who also owned the local pub, would be there later that afternoon. The team sat and made plans for the repatriation of the thugs. Tim was to stay behind with Hannah and keep watch. Tracey rather liked Tim so the arrangement was perfect. The rest of the team would take the Sprinter and Greg's Landrover to Manchester, as well as one driving the BMW X5. Legs drew the short straw for that one. Once at Flaka's house, they would simply dump the four thugs on the driveway and return home. They would leave the Beemer across the driveway and throw the keys away on the way back home. A stalling tactic which might or might not work. A nice simple plan. It would take around three hours. Plenty of time for Tracey to sort Hannah's hair out and have a chat with Tim. In the meantime, the team would patrol the fifty acres looking for weak spots and rectify them. The Guard Commander, a middle-aged veteran named Barry Frazer was an ex RUC Cop, who had served with Greg, Barry got things done. It was rumoured that, one day, he dropped a fifty pence piece off the roof of a car park. He ran down to pick it up and it hit him on the back of his neck! Barry and Greg had been patrol partners on occasion and had saved a few lives.

As they walked, Greg brought Barry up to speed on events so far. Barry assured Greg that no harm would come to Hannah while he drew breath. Greg was satisfied with that. Walking the outskirts of fifty acres is a time-consuming task, especially when stopping to examine potential sniper hides. Barry made note of each one and gave them a number. He was nothing if not organised.

At just after four pm, Tracey arrived at the gate and was ushered through. Greg did the introductions and the girls left to use the bathroom for the hairdo. Pilgrem announced that the thugs were in body bags and ready to go. Their mobile phones had been ringing constantly. Greg smiled.

"I bet Flaka is worried. We'd best keep alert when we get there. I'll go ahead at the last minute and do a drive past. If clear I'll give you the word. Legs, wait until the van is unloaded then throw the Beemer across the drive. Keep the keys, they'll go out later. Then jump into my Rover and we'll high tail it back home. Just in time for a Metaxa eh, Sepp?"

Sepp nodded, "With pleasure."

Back in the house, Hannah was busy putting her new clothes

away. She'd never had this many, even as a child. She sighed.

'I wish Mum could see me now.'

Chapter 10.

Special Delivery.

Dada paced around his spacious living room. Those bungling idiots should have been back hours ago. No answer from their phones made Dada very worried. Flaka would skin him alive if this went wrong.

He called their mobiles again, still nothing. Next he sent a text to George, the Greek he'd put in charge. Nothing to do but wait, he thought. Dada had an exit plan for emergencies and he thought to update it. He contacted his accountant and demanded his funds be transferred to a Swiss bank account immediately. Something did not smell right here, maybe Flaka had met his match? Best to keep his options open. Dada was worth over £5 million. He had that much again in his safe at his office. His yacht was moored in a marina on the south coast, just a few hours drive away. He was tempted to run. Very tempted. A sense of foreboding fell across him and he threw his glass of whiskey away. Decision made; he went to the door. Telling his driver that he'd be staying home, Dada went upstairs and collected his passport and a small folder. His 'insurance'. The folder contained the bank details of every account Dardan and Albana held. Those could be cleared within the hour if necessary but only if Dardan and Albana were dead. The thought of them catching up with him made Dada shiver. Once he'd collected what he needed, he went into the garage and jumped into his average Ford Mondeo and drove to his office. His briefcase soon held all of his money and a small bag of diamonds. Enough to keep him in luxury for the rest of his life. He locked the office door and walked down the stairs to the street. He never made it. Granit snapped his neck in one easy movement, dropped the body the rest of the way down the stairs and collected the briefcase. Flaka had been right. Something had gone wrong on this morning's operation and Dada was sure to run. Granit went straight to Flaka's house with the haul and to report in. His arrival coincided with that of Dada's thugs!

Chapter 11.

Return to sender.

The journey to Manchester had been text book. Greg led the way with the Sprinter second and the Beemer as tail end Charlie. They kept within the speed limits and arrived on the outskirts of Wilmslow two hours after leaving Wales. Greg went ahead to recce Flaka's house. As he slowly cruised along the street of detached houses, he noted a black BMW X5 turn in to Flaka's driveway. Greg slowed as he passed and saw Granit walk into the house carrying a fat briefcase.

'Hmmm' thought Greg, 'wonder why he's here?' He carried on to the end of the road before pulling into the kerb. He called Legs who was driving the Beemer and updated him. They had stopped at a petrol station and Legs passed the info to Sepp and Jack. They then set off to where Greg waited. The team had a chat at the side of the road and took off. The Sprinter pulled quickly up to Flaka's driveway and Sepp and Jack jumped out. From the side door, they dragged four body bags and left them in the drive. Next Legs drove the Beemer quickly across the double gated entrance, jumped out and ran to Greg's Landrover. The

Sprinter and Rover took off at high speed before Flaka had a clue what was happening.

Inside the house, a servant screamed. She ran to Flaka and pointed to the gate.

"Dead men!" she shouted, "Dead men!"

Granit ran through the doorway and to the body bags. For dead men they were moving a lot and making a lot of noise. He turned one over and recognised the face as one of Dada's men. He also noted the note pinned to the outside of each body bag.

"Returned to sender. This time alive. They won't be so lucky next time. Back off!"

"Klysh Kurve!" he exclaimed. It was Albanian for' Son of a bitch'. Taking his knife from his jacket pocket, he cut all four men free then marched them in to see Dardan. Shaking, they told their story. Flaka watched their eyes for any sign of lying, but these men were so traumatised, they could not possibly be lying.

"Granit, take these men, clean them up and pay them for their troubles. They are no longer required."

Relief flooded the men's faces as they followed the giant. An hour later they were taken to Manchester Piccadilly Station, handed a wad of cash and told never to return.

Flaka sat nursing a large brandy. He was in a quandary. The man he called the Crusader was obviously not alone. His backup seemed professional. But pride and the Albanian Code of Honour dictated that he carry on. He had been robbed and dishonoured. To let it go would be to lose face and his reputation in the area would be destroyed. No, he had no choice. However, he could afford to be generous. He would contact this Crusader and offer him a way out. Hand over the girl and Dardan would not destroy him. That sounded fair to the Albanian. He poured himself another brandy and waited. McReanor had been instructed to get this Crusaders background and contact details. They should make interesting reading.

The journey back to Snowdonia was uneventful. Both vehicles took turns to fall behind to keep an eye open for a tail, sometimes as far as two miles. They turned off the road through the village and Greg radioed the gate. As they swung in, the gate slid open and two perimeter guards stood watching. Greg acknowledged them and drove to the house. He and Harry went inside whilst the rest went to the bunkhouse to freshen up. Sav heard them come but stayed lying in the hallway, unusually. Greg stepped inside and stopped dead. There in front of him was the most beautiful sight he had ever seen.

Hannah stood in the hall watching his expression. Her hair had been trimmed and washed. Lipstick and eye shadow had delicately made up her pretty round face, and an electric blue sleeveless dress, down to just above her knees, hugged her shapely figure. Greg felt his jaw drop.

"What do you think?" Hannah asked, tremulously.

Greg hesitated then said,

"I'm sorry, we haven't been introduced!"

Hannah stepped forward and playfully slapped his arm.

"Thank you, that's the greatest compliment I've ever been paid." And reached up to kiss his cheek.

Behind him, Greg heard Harry chuckle.

"I think this is where I make a sharp exit old son!" he said. "I'll check the guys are ok and we'll all come down for a debrief shortly." He turned and left the house, still chuckling.

Greg took Hannah's hands and held her.

"I am honestly lost for words." he whispered. "It's, I mean, you, I mean, simply WOW!"

Hannah beamed,

"It's all down to you, and Tracey of course. She brought the dress and it's a perfect fit. Oh, and by the way, we're all invited to the pub this evening. She's saving us all a table. Wants to know all about what's been going on. She's so lovely."

Greg walked he into the conservatory. Sitting down, he beckoned Hannah to sit next to him.

"I'm not sure that's a good idea" he said, "I'll have to fight every man in the village to keep you away from them!"

Something hit Greg at that moment, he just didn't know it. Cupid's arrow had landed firmly in his heart but, having been single for so long, it didn't register in his mind. As he sat with this vision of loveliness, his eyes were drawn to the picture of another young lady and he walked across to the montage. Standing in front of it, he studied one photo. His eyes watered as he remembered. Without realising it, he whispered,

"I couldn't help you, but I won't fail Hannah. I promise!"

Hannah stayed on the settee, watching him. She didn't speak or move. Then the moment was over and Greg turned to her.

"Yes, we'll go to the pub for a meal. The guys deserve it. I'll invite Barry too. Then, tomorrow night, his team can do the same and we'll cover the security. You look amazing, honestly. But when we come back, I'd like a chat with you. There are some things you need to know."

Hannah looked worried. Greg continued,

"Nothing to worry about. Just some things I need you to know."

Hannah nodded, thinking she had an idea what was coming. It would involve the girl in the photo, Miriam. She realised that it must be very difficult for Greg to tell her what had happened and her heart went out to him. But, she decided, the evening meal would be a fun occasion, as Greg had had enough stress for one day. In the two days since she had met Greg, Hannah had fallen, head over heels. There was an age difference she realised, but no one had ever treated her this way and it felt right. Doubts over Greg's feelings flooded her mind but were interrupted by the noisy arrival of the rest of the team. Tiny Tim had guarded her while the rest had gone to return the thugs and had deliberately kept out of the way when they returned. He knew Greg well enough and had guessed his reaction on his return. That, he had observed from a bedroom door and he was pleased. The debrief should be very interesting!

Dardan Flaka sat in his usual spot in The Albana. His sister, after whom the club was named, sat with him. Flaka's face was not what she expected. There was no angry outburst, rather he looked as though he was respecting his opponent, the one he called The Crusader. And Dardan was relishing the coming fight. Granit and Ismet sat at a nearby table. Granit was brooding. He had a bandage across his nose which had been set by the doctor. He wanted to kill the man who had so humiliated him. When he heard how Dada's men had been returned, he had demanded he be allowed to drive straight to Wales and exact his revenge. Flaka had overruled him.

"This Crusader is skilled, cunning and has a support network. This will take careful handling, not running off here there and everywhere. Sit, shut and learn!" he had snapped.

A waiter came to the table and handed Flaka a sheet of paper. Just the one.

"McReanor left that with the doorman" he said and retreated to the bar.

Dardan read the notes on the paper. Then he read it to Albana.

"So, this man, ex British Army, runs a Security Consultancy. No details on his military record. That means he was Special Forces, may the SAS they have here. So, well trained. Access to many things we don't. There is an address and a telephone number. Albana, get me a vodka, large. I need to plan our strategy."

Albana snapped her fingers and a waiter appeared as if by magic.

"Vodka, large!" she snapped. As the waiter moved away, she called "Bring the bottle. And two glasses!"

The team, along with Hannah, settled at the large glass dining table. Greg told Tim and Hannah what had happened. Tim applauded.

"Nice" he said, "Very nice. So what now?"

Greg smiled,

"I doubt that Flaka will come here for a while. He'll still be reeling. I suspect he'll be looking for info on me. Then he'll make his move. So gentlemen and lady" he nodded to Hannah "tonight we dine at the pub. Harry, can you invite Barry? Then tomorrow night we will be perimeter guards while Barry and his team have a meal and a few drinks on me. Then on Monday we make our first move. I'll not target his drugs dealers just yet. We'll wait for Harry's observation team confirm their movements. Instead I'll let Legs play with his explosives!"

Legs grinned happily. Greg continued,

"Flaka has a warehouse in Birkenhead which holds his imports and exports. There's going to be an accident there on Monday night. The fire brigade will of course find plenty of drugs there. The police will put it down to rival drugs gangs fighting over territory."

Hannah giggled,

"That's great, can I come?"

Greg sat still. That was a question he had not expected.

"Can we decide that tomorrow Hannah?" he asked, "it's not something I want to decide just now."

Hannah nodded, somewhat disappointed.

Greg went off to shower and change, leaving the rest of the team enjoying a well-earned coffee and feet up time. He emerged twenty minutes later, dressed in a cream cotton suit with a white open neck shirt and brown loafers.

Tim wolf whistled,

"Wahoo boss, looking like man at C&A!!"

Hannah laughed, "What is C&A?"

Tim then explained. Greg chuckled,

"Come on then you reprobates, let's go eat. "

Harry volunteered to drive and Legs climbed into the front, leaving Greg and Hannah no choice but to sit together in the back. They smiled at each other, recognising a set up when they saw one. Tim, Sepp, Jack and Barry took control of Harry's Volvo with Tim driving. Harry called out to him,

"Drive carefully you! The misses will kill me if that car gets so much as a scratch!"

Joyfully, after a job well done, they drove the mile to the pub. There were few cars in the car park but the camp site was obviously full. As they walked in the conversation level dropped, mostly due to Hannah. Tracey acknowledged them with a wave and a smile and beckoned them into the bar at the back of the building.

"I've saved you the best table Greg. How does Hannah look now?"

Greg just nodded and said "Stunning. Great job Trace, thanks. I'll settle up in a minute."

"Don't thank me" said Tracey, "When someone is a natural, the job is made much easier."

Greg beamed with pride. Hannah blushed and took in the surroundings, spotting a juke box. She stood and walked across to it then spoke to Tracey. Shortly after, 'Shotgun' by George Ezra boomed into the bar and she and Greg exchanged grins. Then they started to sing along and, pretty soon, all eight of them were singing with gusto. When the song finished Greg and Hannah fist bumped. Barry asked the question that was on everyone's lips,

"What was that all about?"

Hannah explained and they all relaxed. Barry thanked Greg for his suggestion that the perimeter team follow them the next night but said the team had, as one, expressed the wish to remain on site. Greg thanked Barry and promised to put a bonus in each of the teams pay packet. Barry nodded his gratitude. The evening went well and a few hours later they were all back at Llamedos, Greg and Hannah going to the house, Harry driving home after checking his Volvo for damage, and the rest retiring to the bunk house. Sav went outside to do his business before lying on the floor next to Hannah, his big head on his bigger paws.

The discussion between Greg and Hannah was going to be awkward for Greg and he was not looking forward to it. He poured them both a glass of white wine and sat beside this lovely woman.

Chapter 12

"Miriam"

Greg looked at Hannah. There was a strange look in her eyes, sympathy maybe? Or did he detect fear. He tried to smile.

"Hannah, you told us about your life before, well, before we met. It's only fair that I tell you mine. I don't know how you will feel when I've finished. That's a chance I'm having to take."

Hannah continued to look him in the eyes. Greg had felt scared in battle a few times but right now he was petrified. Of hurting this girl and, more importantly, of losing her.

"I joined the army when I was seventeen. Against my parents' wishes. I was a weedy scrawny kid and they gave me two weeks before I came running home. I guess that spurred me on. I joined the Royal Corps of Transport, seventeen years old, five feet ten and seven stone soaking wet! I stayed away from home right through my training and, one year later, visited my parents. I was now over six feet tall, and weighed eleven stone. Lots of gym work had padded me out. They got quite a shock. When I was eighteen I was posted to Northern Ireland on a two-year tour. At the end of that tour I volunteered for another. When my time was up I left and joined the Royal Ulster Constabulary. Big ambitions, small results." He paused, "That's where I met Miriam."

Greg took a sip of his wine, not looking at Hannah. He stood, walked over to the montage and touched the picture of the Pixie-like face. He sighed and took a deep breath. He kept his back to Hannah, unable to see any look on her face. He continued,

"Miriam was a fellow cop. Looked so much like you. Same fire and personality too. I think she lacked your strength though. Anyway, we were just friends, nothing more. We were based in Lisburn, 'slipper city' some called it, but we had our share of trouble."

"Over the next two years we were inseparable. On duty and off. Everyone assumed we were an item but that never entered our minds. I'd have died for her. And, I think, she for me."

Greg risked a look at Hannah. Her eyes were watery. He held her hand, trying to smile.

"I met and got married to Conner's Mum. I think it was to prove to people that Miriam and I were just friends. Miriam was a bridesmaid. Conner was born and then it happened. We were on patrol to what we called 'The High Country', Divis Mountain. A farmer had allegedly called in about sheep rustling. Anyway, we drove there, in a squad car, but unmarked."

He took a deep breath.

"Four IRA terrorists opened fire on us. Our windows were shot out but they missed the engine. Miriam took four bullets, one to the head, but I didn't know that then. I didn't even think of firing back, I just raced down that mountain road to Belfast, the Royal Victoria Hospital. I slammed cars out of the way, I broke every law you can imagine. But when I got there she was dead. I didn't even get to say goodbye. And that hurts."

By now Greg had tears in his own eyes, so he took a deep breath and tried to compose himself. He turned to Hannah and sat next to her. Many was the time he had sobbed himself to sleep since then, but never in front of another person.

"She had four gunshot wounds and I had nothing. Not a damn scratch. I tried to save her. I failed. The next day I handed my warrant card to my Inspector and went home. We packed up and left Northern Ireland the next day. I've never been back. I didn't even go to Miriam's funeral. I was scared I would kill someone. We moved to the Midlands but my marriage failed. I brought Conner here and set up 'The TEAM', a security company. Over the years I won contracts for the Government and here we are."

Greg looked at Hannah. Neither spoke for several minutes. Then Hannah broke the silence.

"Thank you for telling me. Now I understand. You are helping me, and that's all that matters."

Greg gazed into her eyes, seeing a genuine fondness. What she said next took him completely by surprise.

"Greg, I'm part of your life now and I want to be a big part. I'm very fond of you. You're ok, for an old fella!"

Greg burst out laughing, "Less of the old!" he laughed, "I'd like that too."

"And I want to be part of 'The TEAM' too. If you are going into harm's way on my behalf, I want to be there, right by your side."

Greg was stunned. He hadn't given that any thought. He nodded,

"Yes, I think that could be arranged. You'll need training of course, but I don't want you in harm's way." Hannah tried to speak but he held up his hand,

"Please, humour me. I don't want you hurt. I couldn't bear that."

She nodded. "Okay, for now anyway. I'll do office stuff and you can show me how to fire a weapon. One more gun could come in handy you know."

Greg looked at his watch. It was getting late but he didn't feel tired. Hannah asked him how he knew Harry.

"Harry served with me; I was his Sergeant but he had much more experience than I. Harry was in the same Unit as me. But, after a few years, it was clear he had diabetes. Those idiots in the

MoD tried to get rid of him, but you don't keep a man like Harry down. He out foxed them and became a medic. God knows how many lives he saved. He went to the Afghanistan, I didn't. I was long out by then. He ended up a Warrant Officer, well deserved to be honest. He left the army about three years ago and came here. I couldn't do without him. His network of contacts is incredible and he's a great friend. Tim was recommended, as were Sepp and Jack. Legs was sent by a government department. And Barry applied to an advert. The perimeter crew, Barry recruited. We have a good turnover with excellent profit. Some of the guys carry out bodyguard duties, pop stars etc. Sepp and Jack worked for the Rainbow Hospital in Llandudno, both being highly trained Combat Medics. Legs drove ambulances and even Conner worked there, on the maintenance team. Others set up security for people with shed loads of money. It's profitable."

The two chatted for another hour then Hannah yawned.

"I'm sorry" Greg said, "It's either late or I'm boring you!"

Hannah smiled.

"You could never bore me. But, yes I am tired. Can I ask you something?"

"Anything."

"I don't want to sleep alone. Could I sleep with you? Just sleep mind."

Greg nodded.

"I'll use the bathroom then. As long as you promise not to molest an old fella?"

They laughed and Greg turned down the lights. Sav stayed where he was, not even wanting to go outside.

Greg went to the bathroom and brushed his teeth. Looking at himself in the mirror he thought,

'Old fella indeed!'

Then he went into his bedroom, undressed to his boxers and climbed into the bed. He turned off the light, to give Hannah some privacy. She came into the room smelling of lavender and tooth paste. She slid into bed and snuggled up to him.

"Goodnight Greg" she whispered and fell asleep.

Greg smiled. "Goodnight Hannah" he said.

Greg awoke at six the next morning and slid quietly out of bed, taking care not to disturb the still sleeping Hannah. He had slept surprisingly well the previous night given that he had been afraid to move for fear of waking Hannah. He dressed in jeans and t shirt and left the bedroom. Sav looked up at him, almost questioningly.

"Mind your own business pal!" Greg chuckled. Sav walked to the back door ready for his toilet session. Greg opened it and inhaled the cool fresh morning air. A slight mist had settled at the top of the hill behind the house. The sun was trying to penetrate it though, and a good day was promised. He lit a cigarette and watched Sav sniff the grass. He thought back to last night. Hannah had surprised him. He could now see just what guts this girl had and how she had used those attributes to survive in a cold, hard, and, sometimes vicious world. He was proud of her.

Sav came trotting back and Greg gave him a fuss. The dog licked him and ran to get his tennis ball. The two played fetch for a few minutes before Sav decided it was breakfast time. Greg fed him and switched his coffee maker on. As he stood looking out of the kitchen window he heard Hannah enter the room. He turned and smiled at her.

"Good morning sleepy head" he said. She had also dressed in jeans and a t shirt and walked over to him.

"Good morning. Did you sleep well?"

He laughed, "Very, thank you." He paused, "I think we should keep that between just us two?"

"Of course" Hannah replied, a mischievous glint in her eyes. "I have my reputation you know!"

When the coffee was ready, they went into the conservatory and sat together. Greg had his laptop on his knees and they ordered Hannah several sets of combat trousers and other kit she would need. After that they sat in companionable silence, Sav across Hannah's feet. It was almost domestic bliss.

One hundred miles away, domestic bliss was not on the agenda. Dardan Flaka woke at the same time as Greg and in a similar mood. He jumped out of his bed with no thought to the young girl lying there. He slapped her viciously, saying,

"Up and out, fuck off!"

The girl groaned but, realising whose bed she occupied, quickly dressed.

"I need my fix" she said simply. Flaka opened a drawer in his bedside table and threw a packet at her.

"Now go" he snapped. She did as she was ordered.

Flaka went into his kitchen and made a coffee, black no sugar. Sitting at his mahogany breakfast bar, he studied the paper on Greg again. This man would be an interesting adversary. His Achilles Heel would undoubtably be the girl and it was up to Flaka to exploit that. He played the options over in his mind before making a decision. Snatching up his mobile phone, he dialled the number he'd been given for Greg.

'Time to give this Crusader a wake-up call' he thought.

*****

Greg sat checking the work schedule for following month. He made a few changes to the spreadsheet and sighed. This business with the Albanian had come at the right time, work was light for the next ten days. Then it got extremely busy.

Hannah sat reading 'The Dandelion Clock', a book she'd become fascinated by. They sat side by side in silence, making the most of it until the rest of the Team arrived.

The office phone rang and Greg looked at the screen, withheld number. Unusual. He pressed talk and said,

"Speak"

A heavily accented voice replied, "Not a very professional way to answer a call Mr Angel!"

"You don't deserve a professional response, Flaka!" Greg snapped back.

"Do you realise who you are talking to!"

"I know who and what. You are a crook, a thug and a bully, or in plain English, an arsehole," Greg responded, motioning Hannah to remain quiet.

"Klysh Kurve!" Flaka threw back, calling Greg a son of a bitch in Albanian. Greg smiled and replied in the same language, "Temper, temper, you'll give yourself a heart attack, I hope!"

Flaka cursed again. "And here I am making you an offer you would be so stupid to refuse."

Greg stayed silent; Hannah was holding his left hand tightly.

"I am feeling generous. I will give you 24 hours to return my 'asset'. If you do, I will kill you slowly! If not, it will be a long, slow and painful death for you both. You will not survive the storm Angel!"

Greg looked at Hannah before leaning over and kissing her lightly on the lips, whispering, 'over my dead body!'

He spoke rapidly into the phone.

"I AM the storm! You will have my answer within the next 24 hours." Then terminated the call. He cradled Hannah in his arms, looking into her eyes intently.

"Nothing, but nothing is taking you away from me. OK? Nothing.!"

They were sitting holding each other when the TEAM burst in to the house, full of boisterous spirits, which disappeared when they saw the couple. Hannah sobbed gently as Greg stroked her hair. It was Tim who spoke first,

"Boss? What is it?"

Greg told them of the call. The looks on their faces betrayed their emotions. Anger filled the room.

"So what's the plan Boss?" asked Sepp.

"I told him he'd get his answer within 24 hours. He will. This afternoon we take out the factory in Birkenhead, Hannah, you'll come with us. I'm not leaving you here, even with Sav."

The TEAM relaxed slightly.

"Get the two Open Reach vans ready, Legs, and enough overalls for all of us. No firearms though. Baseball bats. Also get petrol and other accelerants ready, in both vans. I want that bastard place to look like a nuke hit it! Harry, get on to your obs team that's covering the drug mules. Detailed movements including their addresses and the last collection they make. We'll hit them tomorrow. We've got a busy couple of days so let's get some food inside us after basic checks, ok?"

All the Team nodded. Hannah raised her hand, like a school child in class.

"Maybe I can sort the food out, if that's ok?" she asked Greg. He took her hand,

"That would be fantastic Hannah, but don't spoil us, especially this lot, they've got pretty basic tastes!"

Hannah laughed, "Basic it is then, now, if you'd let go of my hand, I'll get started."

With that she stood and left the room. Legs went down to the basement to start preparations for the upcoming fire. Sepp and Jack went off to bring the two fake Open Reach vans down from the barn. Pilgrem went to the bunkhouse for the work wear. Harry looked at Greg.

"I'll sort out fake work orders for both vans. I'm sure the security will want to see some."

Greg nodded. "I'll get the baseball bats ready."

Harry hesitated then spoke.

"Greg, is taking Hannah with us the right thing?"

"I'm not leaving her anywhere that she might be vulnerable Harry. Thanks for your concern but that Albanian bastard threatened to kill me and her. Not while I've got a breath in my body. I'll be carrying the Walther PPK, just in case. I'm the only one with a firearm certificate that is legal."

Tim, who had been standing by the window gazing out asked,

"What do you want me doing Boss?" He was keen to get in on the action. Greg looked at the big lad,

"Take the Landrover to the garage and fill her up please mate. Then I want to run through my plan with you and I want you to tear it apart, looking for problem areas. You've got the sharpest tactical mind I've ever known mate."

Tim accepted the compliment with a nod and left the room. Harry and Greg could hear Hannah singing in the kitchen as she busied herself preparing a meal for eight. Harry sat at the computer station and turned towards Greg.

"I'm not prying mate but...."

"Hannah and me you mean? We're close Harry, and that bastard threatened her. I'd be doing the same if any of you were threatened like that. But she's different."

"Like Miriam?" Harry ventured, realising he was treading on thin ice. Greg sat on a settee and said nothing. Harry stood and looked at the photo of Miriam. The differences between Miriam and Hannah were slight and he could see why Greg liked them. He turned,

"Not my business mate, sorry I spoke out"

Greg looked up, "No apology needed Harry, you know that. I couldn't take out the IRA bastards that killed her and that will haunt me forever. But now I *can* stop a thug from ruining any more lives. I, sorry, we are going to destroy his little empire and then I'm going to destroy him. In person."

"And if he destroys you? Where will that leave Hannah? How the hell do you think she will feel? Have you even given that any thought?"

Greg didn't answer, simply left the room. He called Sav to heel and left the house. Turning right, he followed the wall to its turn and then followed that wall too. When he reached the apex of his land he sat on the wall, Sav at his feet, and lit a cigarette. Harry was right. In his quest for justice, Greg had not given a thought to the impact his death might have on Hannah and the TEAM. He smoked slowly, looking around his fifty acres that he'd worked so bloody hard for. Now it was all under threat from some foreign cardboard gangster! Greg's determination was as solid as ever, but now some element of discretion was creeping into his planning. After a second cigarette, he stood and followed the perimeter back to the house. Time to plan.

Chapter 13

The Answer Delivered

Hannah busied herself in the huge kitchen. Having once been a chef, she was familiar with the appliances and soon had the ovens warming up. Greg had said 'basic' so she decided on a brunch for eight people. Well, it was nearly midday. She settled on scrambled eggs with cheese blended in, sausages, bacon, tomatoes, mushrooms and fried bread. As she pottered about, she considered how much her life had changed in such a short time. From hiding in plain sight on the streets of Manchester to living a life of comparative luxury. During the past few weeks she had often dreamt of exacting revenge on Flaka for the misery and pain he had caused her. Now, later today, she was to be a part of that revenge. Flaka had angered Greg and, if what she had seen so far was anything to go by, he would regret that. She smiled and, absentmindedly, sang 'Shotgun', causing her smile to broaden.

Then she thought about Greg. No one could say he was a George Clooney, but he had a rugged handsomeness about him. Come to think of it, none of the Team were fashion model material, but they were beautiful in their own way. And now they were her family.

'What would my Mother say?' she thought, shuddering. 'Too high to even think' Hannah chuckled to herself. She tried to analyse her feelings for Greg. He was her hero, that was for sure. He was strong, kind and protective of her. He's lived a hard life and suffered a great loss and she admired him for that. And, yes, she thought, she did fancy him! A soft pink blush rose to her cheeks. She brushed the thought away. Best get on with the cooking, she thought, still smiling.

Greg and Tim studied the factory in Birkenhead on Google maps, making notes. There was a security hut just inside the wide gates and, beyond, the main building. Google said 50,000 square feet which, Greg remarked, should make a nice glow and have the media running. Tim panned around the perimeter of the building, noting entrances, loading bays and security cameras. Greg and Tim would lead the way in, wearing hard hats, glasses and medical face masks whilst keeping their heads down. Legs and Jack would be in the second Open Reach van and, once the cctv had been disabled, would enter the building with petrol cans. Greg, Tim and Jack would liberally apply the fuel after Legs had placed the detonators. Tim and Greg sat back, satisfied with the plan. The smell of breakfast cooking came flowing from the kitchen and they could hear Hannah singing.

"Hannah sounds happy Boss" Tim said, looking carefully at

Greg.

"Yes, and I'm glad. I know you think bringing her along is risky, but leaving her here is more so. I want her nearby. She will be in the Landrover with Sepp and Pilgrem. We'll take the Motorola radios with us. They can sit at a distance and give us advance warning of any problems. Sound ok?"

Tim nodded. "Yes, it's a good plan. And I promise you Greg, that Albanian bastard won't get within ten feet of Hannah while any of us draw a breath."

Greg shook the big man's hand gratefully.

"Thanks mate. Much appreciated."

As he spoke, the rest of the Team arrived. Legs sniffed appreciatively,

"Hannah, that smells fantastic."

Hannah waved him away.

"Not yet and have you all washed your hands?" she chuckled.

Greg laughed.

"Brothers or not lads, Big Sister has spoken. You know where the facilities are."

They all trooped off, standing in line outside the bathroom while Legs washed his hands. Hannah laughed.

"See Greg, that's how to handle naughty boys!"

When everyone, including Greg, had washed their hands, they all sat at the large dining table and ate. Strangely enough there was no conversation. The TEAM were either too absorbed in the magnificent meal Hannah had created or they were thinking about the operation later that day.

When they had all finished, Greg and Hannah left to smoke while the others loaded the dish washer. The pair smoked in silence, deep in their own thoughts. Occasionally they sneaked a glance at each other and once, when their eyes met, they smiled. Once back inside, the group retired to the conservatory while Tim outlined the plan. When he had finished, Greg said,

"Harry, we need you back here coordinating. Our Motorola's will provide local comms but we'll need to use mobiles to check in with you. We'll each have a call sign, utilising the first letter of our names, so Hannah, you'll be Hotel. Harry, you'll be 'aitch'. Use those at ALL times, even on the phone. No real names. Just in case. Two to a vehicle. Tim and I in the first van, Legs and Jack in the second. Pilgrem, Sepp and Hannah in the 'Rover. Clear?"

They all nodded.

"Right" he continued. It's now 14.00. We'll get into the work clothes, all of us, and set off. Harry, get Barry to have the perimeter guards on high alert while we're out will you? Flaka may have given us 24 hours but he's probably as sneaky a bastard as I am!"

Harry nodded. "Will do. Barry and his crew are itching for some action!"

At that, the Team split up. It did not go unnoticed that Greg and Hannah entered the same bedroom to change into work clothes. Sly smiles were the order of the day. Hannah and Greg changed unashamedly in front of each other and went back to the conservatory. Pilgrem reported all vehicles fuelled and ready to go. Looking the part they left and mounted up. With a wave of his hand, Greg signalled the convoy to move off. They drove swiftly along the lane and turned onto the main road, drawing glances from locals. They bypassed Caernarfon and took the A55 at Bangor. It was plain sailing from then on. Greg and Tim in the lead van set the Satnav for the warehouse in Birkenhead and Tim carried out radio checks with the other call signs. They were tense, as was to be expected, but they were also excited. Hannah sat in the back of the 'Rover and followed everything that went on. She knew Greg was the only one with a weapon and it worried her a little. Gradually she relaxed. Greg was a professional, he knew what he was doing. As the small convoy drove past Chester, she looked wistfully at the city that was once her home. They took the A55 then the A550 and the A41 towards Birkenhead. Greg had decided the M53 was not a viable route there, too many ANPR cameras. As they approached the Industrial Estate where the warehouse was situated, Greg pulled the convoy to the side of the road, next to a Methodist Church. He got out of the van and went back to the Landrover.

"Hannah, can I have a word?"

Hannah stepped out, confusion showing in her eyes.

"Don't look so worried" Greg said soothingly. "I just wanted to say, stay with the Rover and the guys. If we have to leave in a hurry, keep your head down. OK?"

She patted his arm. "Yes, I understand. Good luck. "

They returned to their vehicles and set off. Entering the industrial estate, Greg said on the radio,

"Sierra, this is your watch point, keep engine running. ETR 45 minutes."

"Sierra Roger" replied Sepp and slowed to a stop.

Greg continued,

"Lima, close up, hats on, follow my lead."

"Lima, Roger" came the response.

As they reached the double mesh gates, Greg slowed to a stop and got out, Tim hard on his heels. A security guard in a makeshift uniform came towards him.

"Wassup mate, lost?" he called. Greg carried walking towards the gate.

"Got an order here to check the alarms and cctv mate, orders from," he consulted the sheet on his clipboard, "A Mr Flaka. Marked Urgent."

"I've not been told anything about it mate and everything seems to be working correctly."

Tim stepped forward, towering above the guard,

"Perhaps you'd like to call this Mr Flaka and query it with him?" knowing the guard would do no such thing. Instead the man swung open the gate. Tim and Greg returned to the van, Greg whispering on the radio to Legs,

"Lima, leave Juliet at the gatehouse in case our man gets suspicious. You know what to do."

He drove the van through the gates and up to the main door. He tried the handle and was surprised to find it unlocked. The reason became clear when a second security guard came out, still doing up his jacket.

"Afternoon chaps!" he said, "Call of nature. What are you doing here?"

Greg explained and the guard walked off, satisfied with the explanation. Legs reversed his van up to the main door and waited for Greg and Tim to recce the building. They came back and gave him the thumbs up. The van blocked the view from the cctv but they still kept their hats, glasses and masks on. Neither of the guards were wearing them but that wasn't important. Meanwhile, in the guard room, Jack pretended to check the cctv and asked for the alarm code. Neither of the guards thought this suspicious. Poorly paid, they hoped only to get their pay packet for as little trouble as possible. Jack plugged instruments in and nodded as if all was ok.

"Cuppa?" asked one guard. Jack shook his head and continued working.

In the main building Greg and Tim stood looking around. The aisles of huge packing cases were stacked floor to ceiling. Not one was marked so Greg prized open one.

"Jesus fucking Christ!" he exclaimed. "Fucking look at this Tango!"

Tim walked over and stopped!

"Christ!" he exclaimed and reached into the box. He pulled out an AK47. These took the larger 7.62 cartridges and were lethal in the wrong, or the right, hands. There were ten in the case and Greg counted fifty cases. The two moved from aisle to aisle opening cases. They found hundreds of thousands of rounds of 7.62 rounds, thousands of magazines and cases of military style uniforms, but in black. The three looked at each other.

"Enough here to start, and finish, a civil war Boss!" muttered Tim. "This fecking lot is going to take out half of Liverpool!"

"Tough!" Greg retorted, "Let's see if we can find any drugs. Tim and I will pour the petrol over the weapons and try to avoid the rounds. They'll go up anyway but hey ho. Legs, set 60-minute timers on your little packages. How many did you bring?"

"A dozen, just in case" Legs responded.

"OK, use ten. Scattered around the aisles. Let's get pouring."

It took fifteen minutes to finish the tasks and Greg led the way out. On the way out of the yard, they collected Jack and drove off. Jack's task had been to place a virus in the cctv system at the warehouse. It would only record for ten seconds then automatically wipe all picture. Nothing for the past four hours would be seen on the screen, nor was it stored in the hard drive. Greg radioed Pilgrem,

"Papa, let's get the hell out of Dodge!"

He smiled as he saw the 'Rover tuck in behind Legs' van and they accelerated away. He called Legs,

"Lima, how long?"

"48 minutes Golf"

"Roger." He picked up his mobile phone and called Greater Manchester Police. When the call was answered he asked for Sgt D. McReanor.

"Who shall I say is calling Sir?" asked the young sounding officer.

"Tell him it's 'The Crusader', he'll take my call."

It took two minutes for the Sgt to come to the phone.

"Who is this!" he demanded.

"The Crusader" Greg responded.

"Never heard of ya"

"Flaka has. Call him. Tell him he'll be getting my answer in" he looked at his watch, "41 minutes!"

"What the..!" but Greg had ended the call. He looked across at Tim who was smiling.

"Nice touch Boss!" he smirked. Greg then called Harry.

"Aitch, mission complete. Please keep an eye on local and national news. Tonight's sky should be a bright one!"

Harry laughed.

"Will do. Safe home old son, safe home.

The convoy returned the way they had come. They were nearly home when Harry called them.

"Jesus! What the fuck have you done?" He exclaimed. "It's fucking huge! Explosion in Birkenhead followed by a massive fire. Police report no casualties. Apparently one of the guards, going to the toilet, smelled petrol and evacuated the area. Cops are saying it's part of a drugs war."

Greg smiled.

"Question answered!" he whispered.

*****

Dardan Flaka picked up an expensive Cut Glass Decanter and flung it at the wall of the club, where it smashed into thousands of expensive pieces.

"That fucking bastard!" he screamed, "One million pounds of stock, destroyed by him! I will kill him with my bare fucking hands!"

Granit, never the sharpest tool in the box asked, innocently,

"But, surely it was insured, Boss?"

Flaka strode over to his hired thug, picked him up by the throat and back handed him across the room.

"Insured? In fucking sured you cretin? How the hell could I insure arms, ammunition and drugs you fool?!"

Granit cowered on the floor, wisely not moving an inch. Flaka continued his rant,

"One hundred thousand of these English pounds to the man who brings him to me! Hear me?"

Granit and Ismet left the club which Flaka had ordered closed when the news came in. McReanor had delivered Greg's message but Flaka had not known what to make of it. Now he knew. Albana poured him a large vodka.

"Papa, call off the dogs. I will take care of this Crusader for you. Trust me."

Flaka nodded.

"Get those imbeciles back and tell them to stay around. I may have need of them. Then go, do what you have to. I don't want to know about it until you bring me his head!"

*****

Greg called Pilgrem on the mobile and instructed the call be put on loudspeaker. Pilgrem pulled the 'Rover alongside the lead van and waved. Hannah blew Greg a kiss and smiled. Greg spoke,

"Now listen up folks. We had more of a success there than I hoped." He then told the three what had been found. They all looked shocked. The implication was not lost on them. Potential civil war was a horrendous thing to contemplate. Greg continued,

"Now, Foxtrot is not going to take that lying down. Papa, alert Bravo, I want all his crew on extra high alert tonight. And we'd better stand to as well. Two hours on, two hours off. I'll take first stag with Tim. Get Bravo to call me as well will you? I've had an idea for the drug mules, more when we get home. Now then, Hotel, when we get home, in the cellar there is a chill cabinet. It contains a few Magnums of champagne. I think we've deserved a small celebration but let's not kick the arse out of it, yeah?"

Hannah waved, gave the thumbs up and smiled the biggest smile of her life. Greg felt satisfied but totally alert.

"Drop back again, Papa. Two miles to the rear. Keep alert. Save the celebrations for later."

Pilgrem complied and the conversation in the car was joyful.

Chapter 14.

A 'Royal' Visit.

Police, fire crews and an ambulance remained at the scene of the explosion for many hours. The Detective Inspector in charge, D.I. 'Gore' Downey, stood looking at the carnage. His Sergeant, Paddy Burrows, stood next to him, coffee in one hand, cigarette in the other. Gore was a pedant and proud of it. He enjoyed watching people taking things literally and squirming or backtracking to explain. His nickname came, not from his first name of Gordon, but from the blood and gore he had had on his riot baton, primarily gained from Man City vs Man Utd football matches. Gore was a hard but fair cop.

"What are you thinking Guv?" Burrows asked. Downey kept quiet for a few minutes before answering,

"This is a professional hit. Someone Flaka has severely pissed off. I want a list of his enemies. Oh, and so-called friends too. Anyone who could have done this. I want a trace on those fake Open Reach vans, all the cctv is to be analysed for facial recognition. I want all ANPR cameras checked. I'd guess they came from the Chester direction, more than likely from

Manchester. I also want a list of all the BLM top bods in our area. Counter Terrorist Branch will probably want to take over but this is my area. Are you taking fucking notes?!"

Burrows dug into his pocket for his pocket book and started scribbling. Downey was not one to cross. Just then a squad car pulled up and Sgt Davey McReanor stepped out.

"Oh for fucks sake, what does this prat want?" Downey cursed.

Burrows kept quiet. He hated McReanor with a vengeance but could do nothing about it.

"A bit out of your bailiwick McReanor!" Downey said as the man drew nearer, "Help you with something?"

McReanor smiled, "The owner lives in my area. Sir" he added insolently, "Makes it my business."

"So you can tell me what he stored in there then, being as you know so much!"

"I erm, believe it's his imports and exports Guv" he replied, sheepishly.

"Really?" Downey snapped, "He's a registered arms dealer is he?"

McReanor paled, "What? What do you mean Sir?" he stammered, visibly shocked.

It was Burrows who, rather smugly, supplied the details.

"Hundreds of AK47's and thousands of rounds of 7.62 ammo. Oh, and hundreds of military uniforms, black, the sort of thing Black Lives Matter wear. Know anything about that?"

McReanor stepped back in shock.

"No, I don't. I know he's a crook but arms and ammo? Not his style. Maybe he sub-let?"

The last was more in desperation than anything else. Downey sneered at the uniformed Sergeant,

"You'd best run along now, Sergeant. Maybe report to your master?"

McReanor tensed but backed off when Downey stepped forward,

"We all know you're bent McReanor, all of us. Proof will come, I assure you. Maybe you'll end up sharing a cell with the Albanian mate of yours? Now fuck off, I'm busy!"

Burrows was unable to hide his smile as McReanor stalked off, trying to maintain some dignity. That bastard Flaka! Was he looking to supply a civil war? There seemed no other explanation and McReanor was scared, very scared. He drove away, turning the radio off. He did not want to be disturbed right now. When his mobile rang he ignored it, knowing it was Flaka looking for inside info. Fuck him! McReanor needed to release his tension, and there was only one way to do that with a prostitute, the younger the better.

The TEAM arrived back at the house some ninety minutes after leaving the warehouse. Barry stood at the gate with two of his crew, beaming smiles all around. Greg shook hands with Barry and then they drove to the house.

"Right guys, first things first. Those vans need the Open Reach transfers removing and the correct number plates put on. These overalls, paperwork etc need incinerating in the barn incinerator. Then we all, that's ALL take showers and scrub all residue off. Use the anti- bacterial wash we've all got. Even in the hair. Ok? Right let's move."

He turned to Hannah,

"I know you've not been near the petrol etc, but you need to shower as well. Contamination can cause us problems. I'll go in after you. See you in a minute."

He then went to the basement where he placed the unused PPK back into the gun cabinet. He was relieved not to have used it. And was even more relieved that no one had been hurt. He said a silent thank you to the security guard with a weak bladder.

So far everything had gone off well, but, as any squaddie knows, what can go wrong will go wrong!

Before having her shower, Hannah went into the conservatory to greet Sav. She fussed him then noticed several packages on the settee. Ripping them open she found the combat trousers, shirts and jackets that Greg had ordered. Excitedly she ran to the shower to scrub clean and dress in her new 'work' clothes.

Greg came back upstairs and noticed the wrapping paper and empty boxes. He smiled,

'new clothes always make a woman happy' he mused, 'even work clothes.' He then went into the kitchen to grab a coffee. Barry entered the house and stood in the doorway.

"No problems then Greg?" he asked, leaning against a work surface.

"None, thankfully, but the shit will hit the fan soon enough. Flaka won't take this lying down."

The pair then spent the next ten minutes organising security for the night. All would carry weapons and be ready to use them. Greg and Tim would take the first stag at ten pm and then Greg and Barry would take turns checking the guards. Greg would have Sav with him, his nose was thousands of times more efficient than any humans. Just as they finished, Hannah strode into the room, looking every inch the professional. The uniform fitted snugly and showed off her figure. Greg sighed with satisfaction.

"You look amazing Hannah" he said, and Barry readily agreed. She tried to curtsey but didn't quite carry it off and they all laughed.

"Thanks for these Greg" she said, her eyes showing just how

much the clothes meant. She now felt a real part of the TEAM and it filled her heart with joy. Greg made his apologies and went to shower, scrubbing himself clean then changing into jeans and a t shirt. He gathered up both his and Hannah's overalls and left the house. After depositing the clothes into the incinerator, he invited the other members down to the house for that celebratory drink he had promised, and went there himself.

Barry and Hannah were sitting at the kitchen table, mugs of coffee in hands. Greg motioned Hannah outside and whispered in her ear,

"Champagne!" She trotted off to the cellar and emerged with three magnums of Moet and Chandon, already chilled to perfection, just as the others arrived.

"Now that's timing!" Tim exclaimed happily. "Who is going to open them?"

Greg pointed at Legs, "The explosives expert methinks! His timing was even more perfect. A good job well done one and all, but remember, they will come back at us and we need to be awake and alert."

Legs popped two of the bottles, poured into the champagne flutes Hannah produced and raised his glass.

"To our newest, and of course best looking, recruit. To Hannah!"

Glasses were raised and clinked together and Hannah

blushed. She cast a glance at Greg who was looking at her with pride.

Harry chuckled as he asked Hannah,

"You know Hannah, we've never seen the inside of Greg's bedroom, what's it like?"

As quick as a flash Hannah retorted,

"I wouldn't know Harry; the lights were off!" bringing raucous laughter from all, even Greg. He could see how this enigmatic young woman had survived on the streets for so long. She was as sharp as a razor.

At ten, Greg and Barry took stag, Greg patrolling the northern perimeter, Barry the southern. Guards were positioned at intervals and Sav mooched along with Greg, seemingly relaxed. Hannah was in the conservatory reading what was now her favourite book, The Dandelion Clock. Two of the characters captivated her, Bill and Florrie. Hannah was torn, she wanted to know how the story ended but didn't want it to actually end. No other book had had that effect on her and, as she read, time flew by. Before she knew it, Greg was back from his patrolling and sitting beside her.

"Enjoying the book?" he asked.

"Oh yes!" Hannah gushed, "If you hadn't come home I'd still be reading it. Coffee?"

Greg thanked her and they walked to the kitchen, close

together. Neither felt embarrassed. Hannah wanted to pose a question but was hesitant.

"Greg" she started, then stopped. He looked at her, resplendent in her combats.

"What is it?" he asked gently.

"May I sleep in your room again tonight?"

"Sure, but you realise I won't be there much. I need to keep checking the guards."

Hannah nodded sadly,

"Yes, but you could spend some time with me?"

"I'd like that. But it won't be much I'm afraid. But, yes, we can spend some time together. If you are sure?"

She smiled, "Perfectly sure. Now then, sit down and tell me again what happened at the warehouse."

Greg told her again what had happened. Hannah wondered if Flaka had known what was in there and what his motive was.

"He knew alright and, as a staunch Muslim, it would serve his purpose to have a race war in the UK. He could make more money than even he dreamt of. I'm hoping that the police, or even the Security Services will realise what was in that warehouse and take some form of action. Tomorrow night, we're going to destroy Flaka's drugs trade. Every dealer is going to be rounded up and, let's say, encouraged to leave the area. We will confiscate every penny they have and, by way of compensation to you, will bring it all to you, to do with what you will."

Hannah just looked at him.

"Me? But, can't we help someone else, like homeless teens with it?"

Greg was moved and glad that his initial thoughts had been correct. He put his arm around her.

"You are an extremely rare person, you know that? Most people would have asked 'how much', but your first thought was to help others. Like I say, do with it what you wish. I'm sure Centre Point would be grateful for a donation. Mind, it'll be a lot of money, so maybe do it anonymously?" And then he kissed her, on the lips. He met no resistance and they kissed for several minutes. They sat looking at each other, unsure what to say. The atmosphere was electric until Greg's radio squawked,

"Golf, Gatehouse."

Greg responded and waited.

"Boss, can you come down here?"

It was Terry, one of the perimeter guard.

"Roger."

Greg stood and looked at Hannah.

"Back soon" he said and left the room. He collected his PPK from the cellar and set off to the gatehouse, but not on the track.

He stepped off and circled through the trees, treading silently. As he approached he saw Terry standing behind the gatehouse, shotgun across his elbows but not broken. Something must have spooked him. Greg stepped alongside Terry who didn't move.

"Heard you coming Boss" he spoke quietly. Whispers carry further than low conversation.

"What's up?" Greg asked, casting his glance around but seeing nothing.

"Keep looking at the gate Boss, don't look North or towards the house. Barry labelled potential sniper positions and showed us. His position N5, someone has moved into a sniping position. One person. He's wearing a gillie and all cammed up but I caught the movement. He's hunkered down for the night I reckon. Glad you didn't use the path. I knew you wouldn't."

Greg remained in the shadow, "So what do you reckon Terry?"

"He'll not move tonight; he'd be too easy to catch or shot before he can get away. He's waiting for something. Maybe the perimeter guards should avoid that area?"

"If he's any good that'll spook him. No, carry on as usual, act normal. Pass the word but by mouth, not radio. In fact radio silence from here on in. We'll wait, let him make the first move."

Greg moved off, back the way he had come and slipped into the house via the conservatory door. The sniper would not be able to see him no matter how good his sight was, the glass saw to that. Triple thick, bullet proof and one way. Hannah looked up,

"What is it?"

"Just a false alarm" he said, trying to be reassuring.

"Well, I'm going to bed. Give me five minutes and join me?" Greg nodded, smiling.

Greg waited the required five minutes, fussing Sav. Then he as casually as possible, walked into his bedroom. Hannah was already in bed, sitting up. She was wearing a nightie of crushed silk, white and off the shoulder. The book in her hand was as Greg expected. She looked up and smiled.

"Time for some plain talking I think!" she said. Greg shut the door but stayed where he was. This was alien to him and he felt totally out of his depth.

"About what?" he enquired.

"Us!" Hannah responded, still smiling.

"Oh, yes, us" Greg managed.

Hannah held out her hand.

"Please, sit with me."

Greg did as directed.

"I know we have things to sort out" Hannah started, "But I want to tell you just how much I appreciate everything you have done for me. No one, and I mean no one, has been so kind. I owe you and, if you let me be an integral part of the TEAM, I'll show you how grateful I am. Now, please, for God's sake, kiss me!"

Greg took her in his arms and kissed her, fervently. But that was all. He had a duty to perform and, reluctantly, left her to sleep. As he left the room, Greg turned and looked at this woman he adored.

"Sleep well my love," he said. "Sleep well."

Chapter 15

Sniper.

Shortly after 1 am, two of the perimeter guards, dressed in civilian clothes, climbed in to Greg's MG, lowered the roof and drove to the gate. After some noisy banter with the gate guard, they drove away, waving back. Three miles along the road, they raised the roof and climbed out. In the cover of bushes they donned Ghillie suits and balaclavas. In holsters by their side were Browning Hi Power 9mm pistols. After a look at their surroundings they set off across fields back towards the house. When roughly one mile away from the sniper, they took their pistols in their hands, quietly cocking them and then made a long, slow, laborious crawl to the sniper's lair. The night was moonless and chilly. Stars gave some ambient light but not enough to see them by. Three hours later, they were within touching distance of the sniper and he had no idea they were there!

*****

Barry had insisted that Greg get some sleep. After one last tour around the grounds, even going near to the sniper, Greg had reluctantly climbed, fully dressed, into bed alongside the sleeping Hannah. Within moments he was sound asleep.

Hannah woke him just after six o'clock with a cup of black sweet coffee. He sat up groggily and thanked her. She had dressed in her combats again and Greg was pleased. They chatted for a few minutes before Greg decided to make a move. He stood and Hannah hugged him tightly.

"What do you think they'll do Greg?" she asked, looking worried. Greg then explained about the sniper but told her not to worry as everything was in hand. He smiled confidently and Hannah was reassured.

The pair had a light breakfast in the conservatory. Sepp, Jack, Legs, Tim and Pilgrem had all been on stand to during the night and were looking forward to a sleep but Greg asked them to wait. He had a feeling something was about to happen and he wanted a full TEAM for when it did.

*****

The powerful motorbike rolled slowly into a layby a mile from Llamedos, the rider wearing all black, including the helmet. Even the visor was heavily tinted. Her long black hair hung between her shoulders as she waited. Her mobile phone pinged once, indicating she'd received a text message. She read it and smiled,

"In position" it read.

She accelerated back onto the road and headed for Greg's house. Once on the track she revved her engine hard, making sure that her sniper could hear and then drove up to the double gates.

Greg sat in the conservatory watching the gate. Four of the guards, armed with shotguns, approached the lone rider and signalled her to dismount which she did. She then took off her helmet and smiled.

"I have come to see The Crusader" she said. Greg had to admit, Albana was a looker and he could see that the guards were impressed as well. He grabbed his radio,

"Gate, send our guest up to the door" he ordered. Hannah gasped,

"That's Albana! Be careful, she's very dangerous. She has killed men and women. Please Greg, don't let her near me!" she said, panicky.

Greg put his arm around her and hugged.

"Relax, I promise it's alright. Come, we must make our guest welcome" and, taking her hand, he led her to the door. Sav was there already and growled. Hannah stroked him and he stood beside her.

"Alert!" Greg ordered the dog and Sav stepped forward, hackles rising, a deep growl in his throat as the motorbike slowly approached.

Albana dismounted and made to walk forward but stopped when Greg produced his PPK and pointed it at her. She stopped and glanced to her left, North, towards where the sniper lay. Greg raised his left hand in a signal. The two guards in Ghillies pressed the barrels of their pistols to the sniper's temples and ordered him to stand. When all three were standing, Greg looked at Albana.

"Look to your left Albana. Your sniper is one step away from being dead. And so are you. You see, over to the East is a sniper of my own. He has never been known to miss. So, state your piece and fuck off!"

Albana pointed at Hannah,

"I want the girl. She does not belong to you. My father wants her to work for us." She was angry and her Albanian accent had become more pronounced. Albana had been outflanked by this man. It was becoming a habit, one that she needed to break. Her Father would be furious when he found out.

Hannah showed remarkable courage by stepping forward.

"No one owns me you bitch!" she snapped, "Your Father is a pimp, a bully, a thug and an arsehole. You take after him."

Albana cursed in her native tongue and Greg replied in the same. That shocked her.

"Where did you learn my language?" she asked.

HANNAH

"Not in the same gutter as you did" Greg replied smiling. "You've had your answer. I hope the warehouse wasn't too badly damaged?" This caused a burst of laughter from the TEAM who had stood to one side, letting Greg own the show.

"You bastard! You will pay for this!" Albana fired back, "Am I to be allowed to leave, unharmed?"

Greg looked at Hannah who was standing glaring at her enemy. She looked back at Greg and nodded. Greg spoke,

"Albana, you have Hannah to thank for your life. If you think for one minute that, had she shaken her head, I wouldn't kill you, think again. I will kill *anyone* who tries to hurt Hannah, and that includes stuck up bitches like you! Now get the fuck off my property, and take your sniper with you!".

"Keep him, he's no use to me any longer!" she snapped and strode her motorbike. Donning her helmet she gave Hannah two fingers and roared off.

"Gate. Let her go." Greg said into his radio.

The two perimeter guards arrived a few minutes later with the hapless sniper. Greg looked at him,

"How did you get here?" he asked. The man replied in a Scottish accent,

"They dropped me off last night. There are two more in a car along past the pub. I'm supposed to text them when I've killed you."

Greg invited the sniper into the house and offered him coffee.

"Coffee before you kill me?"

"Don't worry, I'm not going to kill you. Mind, Sav here will if you make a sudden move, ok?"

The man, who told them his name was Joseph, nodded and backed away from Sav slowly. They all sat around the table.

"What next Joseph?" Harry asked.

"I don't know. My reputation is in shreds now. I was a sniper in the Para's for ten years. Your guys are bloody good, I had no idea they were there."

Greg came to a decision.

"Pilgrem, get the 'Rover. Then, when he's finished his coffee, take him to Bangor station, put him on a train." He turned to Joseph, "Is that ok? I'll give you money to make a new start but, be warned, if you ever come looking for trouble again, I'll kill you. Got that?"

Joseph nodded and thanked them all.

"You know what? Flaka and that psychopath daughter told me you had kidnapped this wee girlie and we were rescuing her. Seeing her all dressed up in combats, well, it's pretty fecking obvious that bitch lied to me. Here's my number. If I can help in any way, just call. I owe you."

Greg went to his safe and took out £1000 in used notes and handed it to Joseph. With the money was Greg's mobile phone number. The sniper's eyebrows shot up,

"Ah cannae accept that much!" but Greg waved him away. "Safe journey Joseph. Don't worry about the other two. We'll deal with them. You now have my number, if you need me, just call." And with that, Joseph and Harry left the room.

By the time Greg, Legs and Sepp reached the layby the two thugs had left. Albana must have tipped them off.

Greg sent the Team away to get some sleep. Meanwhile he sat with Harry to discuss the drug dealer's plan. Harry would contact his crews that were watching the mules. That evening, when the final collection of money had been completed, two of Harry's men would grab them, tie them, gag and hood them and throw them into the back of a van. The money would be taken from them but the drugs would be left. These men would then be dumped, along with their drugs outside the Manchester Arena and an anonymous call made to the police. The crews would wait nearby to see the reaction. Notes stating 'Drug Dealers Get out of Manchester' would be pinned to their clothing. They were not to be harmed. Harry agreed. Five mules needed five pairs of his men. It was a matter of minutes before he confirmed that all was in place. He then went home to grab some well-earned sleep himself, leaving Greg and Hannah alone. Greg sat on a settee in the conservatory with Hannah by his side. He felt his eyes drooping and, before he could stop himself, drifted off to sleep.

Several hours later Greg awoke. Hannah's head was on his shoulder and she too stirred. They smiled at each other.

"Had enough excitement for one day?" Greg asked.

"Yes, I think so, thank you very much! Greg, what you did for Joseph, it was lovely but he would have shot you if the guards hadn't got to him."

Greg thought carefully about his reply.

"Sweetheart, yes he would. Let me tell you a story. After Hitler killed himself in WW2, a group of influential French were being held hostage in a Castle in Austria. A Wehrmacht Major, Josef Sepp Gangl didn't agree with this. The guards were all SS. Gangl went to the Americans and, along with a Captain Jack Lee, freed the hostages and fought off the SS. Gangl was shot by a sniper as he tried to help one of the Frenchmen. Sepp is directly related to that Major. So you see, there is honour in war, just not very often. Oh, and by the by, Jack is directly related to Captain Jack Lee. That's probably why they are inseparable."

Hannah absorbed this information.

"I am in esteem company then Greg" she said softly, in awe of at least two of her new 'brothers'.

"We both are Hannah, we both are."

Chapter 16.

Tornado.

Albana stood in the doorway of her fathers' house, nervous for the first time in her life. She had to explain her failure to Flaka and he did not accept failure, from anyone. Using her passcode, she entered and looked around. The palatial hallway was filled with precious works of art. Mahogany walls were highly polished. Subtle lighting cast a pale light on the furniture.

Flaka was sat at his home desk, head in hands. He looked up as she entered but immediately looked down again. His pain at her failure was plain to see.

"Papa" she started, but he waved her quiet.

"Sit" he commanded. When she sat in a plush chair opposite his desk he looked up and spoke.

"I do not blame you for failing. I know you have failed because you did not call with good news. Talk to me. What happened?"

Albana spoke for several minutes, giving Flaka the full

details. He listened carefully and made a decision.

"That one girl has caused me enough trouble. Enough. We know where she is and can go after her at our leisure. I will think about this. They will be looking over their shoulders forever. That is, at the moment, good enough. However, we have a bigger problems. The Brotherhood are not happy at losing the arms and ammunition. They demand we replace. DEMAND! Of ME! Bastards! But I have no choice. The authorities are now aware of the contents of the warehouse although they are keeping it from the media which is on our side."

He paused, watching her face.

"We need to make contact with the supplier again. You do anyway. After all, he is your lover!"

Albana looked at Flaka in surprise.

"Oh, don't deny it, my dear child" Flaka laughed, "I keep telling you, I know everything."

Albana recovered her composure and smiled tightly.

"I haven't seen him for days, Papa"

"Then call him. I want him here, tonight!"

Then he smiled again and poured them both a very large vodka.

"Our enemies will think I am weak now and may try to take advantage. I will call McReanor and tell him to keep his ears to his ground, eh? Drink my child. All is not lost."

They toasted each other and Albana sat musing. She looked forward to reuniting with Salim. She almost laughed out loud as his name translated as 'peaceful'! A less peaceful man she had yet to meet and he was magnificent in bed! She took her Apple iPhone S from her Prada handbag and pressed number one. Salim was on speed dial, obviously. He answered almost immediately.

"My lovely Albana, how are you?" he oozed. He had many reasons for being nice to Albana, sex being only one.

"My sweet" Albana replied, "I haven't seen you for days. Have you forgotten me?"

"Always on my mind, my sweet" came the smooth reply, "When can we meet again?"

Albana knew he was hooked and reeled him in.

"Why, I'm free tonight my lover. Why don't you come to the house, say seven o'clock? Papa would so like to meet with you. Then, after, we can entertain ourselves".

Flaka winced. If Salim was staying, Flaka was going out, all night! His beautiful daughter's love life held no fascination for him.

The date arranged, Albana ended the call.

"Papa, I must shower and change. See you later." And left the room.

*****

GCHQ in Cheltenham is a government intelligence and security agency founded in 1919. It monitors signals intelligence and keeps the UK safe from terrorists. Or at least tries to.

The operator who listened to the call between Albana and Salim called his superior, who passed the information up the ladder until it stopped. Right at the desk of the Head of MI5. Sir Dickie Gerrard-Wright was an ex-army General, often described as a 'boots officer'. There are usually two types of officer in the British Army. Shoes and boots. 'Shoes' officers are Staff Officers who rarely take their feet out from under their desks. 'Boots' officers are generally well liked by the troops and officers alike. Dickie had served in the Gulf, the Falklands and Northern Ireland where he gained respect from senior politicians from both sides. He studied the signal with interest. He stroked his 70's pop star moustache and looked at the attractive woman who sat opposite him.

"Any thoughts, Jenny?" he asked casually.

Jenny Carpenter was the first woman to head 22 Special Air Service, or SAS as they were more commonly known. At the age of thirty-two she had reached the rank of Major before Dickie had head hunted her. Not just good looking, Jenny was tenacious, intelligent and hard as nails. A Black Belt in Karate, she had also studied Krav Maga with the Israeli Defence Force, beating their own champion twice in succession. Her blonde hair, curvaceous figure and Dresden China Doll face made her stand out and she had had to fight extremely hard to get where she was. During Selection at Hereford, the Staff Instructors initially gave her hell but soon learned to respect her. As a young Second Lieutenant, she had passed with flying colours and was recommended for promotion straight away. Two years with the SAS went by peacefully and she moved on to the Intelligence Corps which is where she was spotted by the then Lieutenant General Gerrard-Wright. Jenny became great friends with his wife, Sue, yet another vivacious blonde with a will of iron. When Dickie became Head of MI5, he sought her out and offered her the job of Director of Military Intelligence. Jenny jumped at the chance to serve with a man she admired tremendously. Jenny had never married, rather she was wed to her job of keeping Britain safe from terrorism. She studied the signal and raised her eyebrows,

"Salim? Cultural Attaché for the UAE Embassy? Hmm, him and the beautiful Albana would be a formidable match. I sense you have something else to tell me?"

Dickie smiled,

"Always sharp dear Lady. Yes, it appears that Angel has had a run in with Dardan Flaka. And Flaka came off second best!"

Jenny laughed, "Doesn't everyone?"

"If memory serves, you matched him pretty well in the Krav Maga stakes here?"

Jenny thought back. That description was not how she remembered it. Greg Angel had appeared to hold back until she delivered a cruel blow to his throat and then he let rip, destroying her completely.

"Thanks Dickie for being kind." Jenny was one of the few to address him by his first name but never in public.

"Well, I think you should have a chat with Angel. I don't want him getting in too deep."

"Is any depth too deep for Angel?" Jenny asked with a smile.

"Down Girl!" Dickie replied, "It seems he's got himself a lady friend. A former homeless girl he rescued from Flaka. Hence the run in. Flaka lost an asset, went to retrieve her, got a bloody nose. I suspect Angel was involved in the warehouse debacle. Destroyed Flaka's stock of arms and ammo he was holding for The Brotherhood. And, knowing Greg as we do, I suspect he won't stop there unless given an order. That, my dear, is up to you!"

Chapter 17.

Reunions.

Greg sat with Hannah and Harry in the conservatory waiting. Waiting for news from Manchester. They spoke little and Hannah kept them replenished with coffee and food. The rest of the TEAM were either still sleeping or eating their own meals. Sav lay by the door, content that all was well.

Harry broached the subject first.

"So what are you two going to do when this is all over?"

The atmosphere was broken by a call to Harry's phone. He snatched it up and listened for several minutes. After ending the call, he looked at Greg.

"It seems a group of vigilantes called, rather ostentatiously, Drugs out of Manchester, or DOOM, have intercepted several of Flaka's drug mules, robbed them and left them bound by ropes near Manchester Arena. They left the drugs for the police to find. How rather unfortunate!"

Harry, Greg and Hannah burst out laughing!

"DOOM," Greg said, "so after BOOM comes DOOM! Flaka will be having a pink fit! Hannah, champagne I think?"

"Oh not for me Greg," said Harry, "I must drive home and spend some quality time with the missus. But thanks anyway.

Greg told Harry to get Barry to release half of his perimeter crew. Flaka would be too busy now to worry about him and Hannah and they could cope with anything that arose. Then he showed Harry out. When he returned, Hannah was sitting with her legs under her, looking pensive.

He sat next to her.

"By the way, as of this evening, you are richer to the tune of £80,000. To do with what you wish."

Hannah looked at him, shocked. She simply could not speak. The amount was incredible but she knew that Centre Point would receive the lions share and was glad. Silence descended on the room, neither daring to speak. In the end it was Sav who saved the day by trotting to the door. He needed his ablutions and so Greg and Hannah went with him. They each smoked a cigarette but still said nothing. They walked side by side, not touching.

As they came to the bunkhouse they heard voices and so went inside. Sepp and Jack were stripped to the waist and arm wrestling. A silence fell over the room when the pair entered but Greg waved them to continue.

The duelling pair sat at a table and took their stances. It was a titanic contest which Sepp narrowly won. He looked at Greg, a challenge in his eyes. Greg took his place and they joined hands in combat. Sepp's arms bulged as he took the fight to Greg but Greg was not easily beaten. For over forty seconds it seemed as if neither would win when, suddenly, Greg slammed Sepp's hand to the table. A roar of appreciation went up. The pair shook hands. Greg spoke,

"Guys, I want to thank you all for the past couple of days. You have proven yourselves yet again. I will be eternally grateful. However, being as Flaka has other problems, it's back to normal." A collective groan rose up and Greg raised his hand. "Trust me, I have some very lucrative contracts coming up but, "here he paused dramatically, "you have deserved a holiday. Come see me tomorrow and tell me your desired destination and I will book your holiday. On me!"

A massive cheer replaced the groan and backs were slapped. Hannah and Greg left the men to their own celebrations. Greg asked, "Have I upset you?"

Hannah stopped and looked at him.

"No Greg, you haven't. It's just that, after all this excitement, I want to know where we go from here. That's all."

Greg took her in his arms.

"Well, I thought we'd do some serious shopping. Sort out your paperwork for ID etc, maybe catch a suntan and generally laze around for a while. You see, Flaka may be busy elsewhere but he sure as hell isn't going to give up. It'll be personal and Albana will want to be involved. So, we need to be careful. But I'm damned sure you are going to relax and have some fun!"

They strolled to the house, arm in arm. Both felt strange, sort of at peace but waiting for a storm to break.

It was getting late and the couple sat in the conservatory. Greg had a thought.

"I'd best ring Conner" he said, "He doesn't know I've found you yet."

Hannah snuggled into him.

"Good luck" she whispered, "Shall I leave you alone?"

"No, please stay. I need you here with me for Dutch courage!"

He picked up his phone and dialled his son. After a few seconds Conner answered in true Conner fashion,

"Hello old age pensioners home, when would you like a room!"

Greg laughed, "Cheeky twat!" he said while Hannah was convulsed with laughter.

"How you doing Son?" he asked.

"Oh I'm ok, you know, the usual. I hear things have been a bit lively up there?"

"I wouldn't know mate; I don't watch the news. Anyway, I thought we'd pop down to see you?"

"We? Don't tell me you've got a woman? Where does she keep her white stick and does her dog get on with Sav?" Conner laughed!!

At which point Hannah could contain herself no longer and roared with laughter. Greg too was in stitches. He had always had a great relationship with his son.

"Hannah?"

"Yes son, Hannah."

"Holy shit you found her? Christ! I knew you would. How, when, where? Tell me all!"

Greg relaxed and winked at Hannah.

"When I see you mate. She's here, listening."

Conner went all serious.

"Dad, I hoped this would happen. Now look after her!"

Hannah chuckled and took the phone from Greg.

"And I'll look after him Conner. Your Dad is a wonderful guy, for an old fella anyway!"

Conner roared with laughter,

"I think we're gonna get on just fine Hannah, just fine!"

They arranged to meet up soon. Greg and Hannah would

drive down to the Midlands and they would have lunch together. Then they ended the call. Greg heaved a sigh of relief. He was glad that was over. Hannah checked Greg's face before speaking.

"Conner didn't seem that surprised."

"No, he wouldn't be. You see, he knows me better than anyone else. Except you, now. Not much I do will surprise him these days."

They hugged and then decided it was time for bed. Sav stayed on his bed in the corner, watching them both carefully.

Yet again, the pair slept alongside each other, occasionally hugging but no other physical contact. It seemed as if there was an unspoken agreement to wait until the time was right.

They awoke next morning at about six o'clock. After a leisurely coffee they went outside with Sav for a cigarette. They sat in a garden hammock gazing around. Hannah broke the silence.

"I thought it always rained in Wales?"

Greg chuckled, "Don't jinx it. We'll get rain soon enough. Mind, a few years ago, a storm with your name arrived here. We had a four-day power cut but we were ok. Conner got a couple of retired people up here and we fed them. Actually, it was great fun. As you can see, we're well stocked for every occasion. More coffee?"

Hannah smiled and nodded. "It's peaceful here. I like it.

What are we doing today?"

"Well, after we send the boys on their holidays, I thought we'd go to Birmingham for shopping, and to see Conner. We'll take the Rover, more room for all your new clothes!"

Seeing the TEAM approach, the pair went indoors and Greg sat at the computer. Hannah greeted the lads and Greg called out,

"Wheel them in Hannah, then they can all bugger off!"

Legs was first in and Greg sorted him a holiday to South Africa. Sepp and Jack followed, a week in Austria was their preference. Pilgrem decided to go home to the Midlands. They said their goodbyes and left, each in their own car.

Greg looked at Hannah. "Right my lovely" he said in a poor attempt at a Welsh accent, "Shall we pop off to Birmingham?"

Laughing, they left the house and walked hand in hand to the car. Just as he unlocked the Rover, his phone rang. Greg sighed, "Sorry Hannah, better take this."

The number had been withheld and Greg was curious.

"Hello?" he said,

"Angel old chap, how the devil are you?" a well-spoken voice called,

"General" Greg

"All well in Welsh Wales?"

"Very, thank you General" Greg said as politely as he could

manage. "Was there something you wanted?"

The General chuckled, "Just to give you the heads up. You're about to have a visitor."

Greg looked around but saw no one.

"And who might that be, Sir?" he asked.

"Jenny Carpenter." The General replied waiting for a response. Greg was curt,

"Why?"

"She needs to have a chat. Nothing too serious, just a sort of 'advice' session."

"When?"

"Within the hour old chap, you know how she drives."

Greg looked at Hannah who had been listening. He saw disappointment on her face and his heart melted.

"One moment General"

He turned to Hannah,

"Sorry, really I am." Hannah nodded and tried to smile, "Don't worry, there's always tomorrow."

"Is that the lovely Hannah, Angel?" the General chuckled.

"Yes General, you've interrupted a shopping trip. A bit more notice in future!" and with that he terminated the call. They walked back to the house in silence. Then Hannah brightened up.

"So tell me about this friend of yours, what's she like?"

Greg looked at her,

"Jenny is not exactly a friend. If I were still in the army she'd be my boss. Trouble is she still thinks she is. She's the Director of Military Intelligence at the MoD. As hard as nails and dirty with it. Ex SAS believe it or not. We're like chalk and cheese."

Hannah chuckled,

"Oh well, in that case, I'm off for a shower, and a change of clothes." She slipped away smiling to herself. This meeting could be interesting.

Greg went to the conservatory and informed the gate guard of his impending visitor. He had neglected, deliberately, to tell Hannah of Jenny's nickname, 'Tornado'. She would arrive, destroy everything you held dear, and then swan off without a care in the world.

He heard the shower and tried to relax, but the feeling of trouble would not go away. About half an hour later he saw a black BMW i8 arrive at the gate. The guard spoke to the blonde driver and waved her through. Greg took a deep breath and stood. As he turned, there was Hannah in the doorway. Hair shining, eyes glinting and a sublime smile on her face. But it was the dress she was wearing that set his pulse racing. She wore a short, diaphanous, halter neck dress, in a silky white, with large blue floral print. It was partially transparent, but totally alluring. He held his breath.

"Oh my God!" he finally managed. "Oh my God!"

Hannah beamed, "Shall I make coffee for us and our '*guest*'?"

Greg could only manage a nod and she went into the kitchen. Greg went to the door, Sav behind him, growling softly. He did not like Jenny and was content to show it. Greg opened the door and motioned Sav to sit. He did, but still growling. Jenny emerged from her latest expensive gift to herself. It had cost over £110,000 and she'd paid cash. Not bad if you can get it. Greg tried to smile, but failed. Jenny was wearing a conservative two-piece trouser suit in navy blue. No tights but her white blouse shone in the sunlight.

"Greg!" she oozed, "Long time eh?" Sav's growl got louder. "Oh I see you've still got that mutt. Oh well, I guess you need some company."

Hannah called from the kitchen, "Sav, here!" and the dog trotted off happily. Jenny raised her eyebrows. "His Masters voice eh?"

Greg led the way into the kitchen where Hannah stood leaning against the sink, eyes boring into Jenny's.

"Ah," said Jenny, "this must be the little homeless girl you rescued. How quaint."

Greg was not prepared for what happened next. Hannah reached behind her and picked up a saucer of milk and handed it to Jenny.

"This should suit you better than coffee?"

Jenny placed the saucer on the table and smiled.

"It seems I've *almost* met my match! I'm Jenny, and you must be Hannah. My, the General failed to tell me just how beautiful you are. I will talk to him about that. Now then Greg, we need to talk. But maybe not in front of a civilian?"

Greg grinned,

"I'm a civilian, and Hannah is now my business partner, so, anything you have to say, Hannah can hear. Is that alright?"

Jenny blanched. How the hell did this homeless waif get so close to this man? She continued,

"oh well, so be it. Coffee first though I think Hannah?"

Hannah smiled an angelic smile,

"It's in the pot over there. Feel free to help yourself!"

At this point, Greg was almost beside himself with pride for Hannah. Any woman who could verbally best Jenny, was, in his book, admirable.

They sat at the kitchen table, Hannah alongside and, very close to, Greg. It did not go unnoticed. 'Claiming her territory' Jenny thought, 'not that I blame her.'

Jenny looked at Greg.

"Greg" she started, "you may think you know all about Flaka but I'm afraid you don't. Let me put you both in the picture. Last night, Dardan and Albana Flaka had a meeting with one Salim Sheikh-bin-Alban, currently Cultural Attaché for the UAE Embassy. The connection between Albana and Alban is not a coincidence. They are, in fact, distant cousins but neither are aware of this fact. Yet!" She paused, "Hannah, you had a very lucky escape, trust me. Greg here did you one massive favour by rescuing you, but he also upset our little apple cart. Thanks to our listening devices, planted about a year ago, we have been tracking Flaka and Salim. You may be aware of allegations that the Saudi's sponsored the 911 attacks?" They both nodded, although Hannah only did so because she believed it was expected of her. Whilst she did remember the attacks, she had no idea who had put up the money.

Jenny continued.

"No proof has ever emerged. For some unknown reason, bin-Alban dislikes the UK. He got his job not just because of his family but because he is one sharp individual. Hannah, no disrespect to you, but Salim would have bought you and shipped you off to the Middle East as a prostitute."

Hannah shuddered and held Greg's hand, under the table. Greg squeezed her hand to reassure her. Jenny was actually quite touched; she had noticed the movement. Greg's face was stony, not a good sign as far as Jenny was concerned. She continued with her report.

"Greg, by rescuing Hannah, you've ballsed up our plans. The arms and ammo you destroyed were bait."

Greg made to protest but Jenny waved his comments away.

"We know, Greg, we know!" she snapped at him, watching his anger rise.

"How?"

"The warehouse was under surveillance too. A guard going for a piss didn't raise the alarm. We did. Just as well, as you'd have flattened Anfield, although that's not such a bad thing!" she chuckled, drily. Both Greg and Jenny had leanings towards the better club on Merseyside, Everton.

"Calm down Greg, let me finish" Jenny said. Greg tried to relax but the thought of 'his' Hannah being used by such people filled him with loathing. He nodded to Jenny.

"Carry on" he said quietly.

"Salim-bin-Alban wishes to start an uprising in the UK. Hence the warehouse. Those boat people arriving in Dover? 95% fighting age men and our pathetic Government put them up in five-star hotels, passing them off as NHS workers? Part of Salim's army. Scattered across the UK, they would be ready to answer the call and fight for their Allah. To take over the UK and turn it into a Caliphate. Salim must be stopped, but, not officially. That, Greg, is where The TEAM come in. Unofficially of course."

She rested there and sipped her coffee. "Lovely coffee Hannah. Thank you."

Hannah was too stunned to answer. What she had just heard scared her but for one thing. Greg. Just then she realised that she loved Greg. Totally. She looked at him and saw his eyes. 'He loves me too!' she thought. It was Greg who broke the silence.

"So, Jenny, where do we go from here?"

Jenny pondered the question.

"I need to liaise with the General. I will let him give you the plan. But for Greg only. Sorry Hannah."

"No fucking way!" shouted Hannah. "Greg saved my life. Where he goes, I go, OK?!"

Jenny smiled, patronisingly,

"But you are not trained Hannah, yet, anyway. I think I can see a role for you but you will need training."

Greg leapt in there. "I will train her."

Hannah smiled. Jenny thought for a few moments before replying.

"Hannah, if Greg trains you, you will be well taught. But you've never killed anyone, have you?"

Hannah shook her head and replied,

"No, but I would if anyone tried to hurt Greg. Is that enough?"

Jenny shook her head,

"No, it isn't. This isn't ancient Greece. I'll let Greg explain things to you later, in the meantime, I'll put the proposal to the General. He and Greg go way back. In the meantime, here's what we are planning. "She then went on to outline her ideas, which would involve Greg and the TEAM, all of whom were on holiday just then. Jenny acknowledged that and said her plan could wait seven days, but no longer. Greg agreed. It would give him seven days to train Hannah, not enough, but a start. Jenny also said that The General wished to see Greg, and, now, Hannah in person. The meeting was arranged for the next day, in London. Hannah was excited as she'd never been to London before. Greg smiled,

"We'll go in the MG then, and take in the sights, eh?"

Hannah hugged him, totally oblivious to the fact that Jenny was still there.

"Well," said Jenny, "That's all arranged then. I'd best be off. Long journey etc,!" she smiled.

"One last thing though. Hannah, I'd like to apologise for my attitude when I first arrived. I had no idea of the sort of person you are. You are a survivor, six years on the streets has honed your instincts. Now you know the sort of person Greg is, I hope you will stick around. And to you both. Listen carefully."

They looked at her intently. She continued,

"You are made for each other! And that is a compliment to you both. You, Hannah, have done something no other female has done, in my memory. You have captivated Greg and I applaud you. Since, well, Greg knows, I've been worried about him. Now I can stop worrying."

Greg was stunned.

"Jenny" he said, "I've told Hannah about Miriam."

"Good. No secrets then. Onwards and upwards eh?"

She stood to leave. Sav growled.

"Oh, for fucks sake dog! I'm a friend, ok?" Jenny laughed, as Hannah called Sav to her and stroked him.

"Sav" she said, "Jenny friend, friend, ok?"

Sav gazed at her then walked over to Jenny and sat by her. Jenny stroked him and he enjoyed the contact.

"Well, if that doesn't beat all, Greg. Remarkable, absolutely remarkable young woman. "They all shook hands and, as they went to the door, Greg held Hannah's hand. Jenny smiled,

"I suspect The General is going to like you, Hannah, I really do! Au revoir people!" and she sashayed off to her car. With a roar, she took off down the track to the gate and flew through it as Greg and Hannah looked on.

They went into the conservatory and sat together on a settee, facing the high, wide windows. The view today was spectacular. Steam trains puffed to the summit of the mountain; light fluffy clouds littered the blue sky. Shadows were cast on the hills and valleys. Neither spoke for a few minutes, then Greg apologised,

"I'm so sorry Hannah" he said quietly, "our shopping trip seems to be abandoned." Hannah leaned into him,

"No problem" she said, "we have lots of time." She gazed into his eyes, "Let's go for a walk. I'm sure Sav would like that."

They stood, and, as if understanding, the dog trotted to the door, tail wagging excitedly. Once outside, they simply let Sav take the lead, the happy couple following on. Overhead, Greg pointed out to Hannah a family of buzzards. They often landed on the wall near the house and Greg was fascinated by them, he told Hannah. The birds circled and shrieked as the couple looked skywards. It was a very relaxing moment. Hannah broke the silence,

"So, when do I start my training?"

Greg chuckled, "Keen, eh? I like that. Well, I have a surprise for you, let's walk down to the gate." They turned and strolled casually along the winding track and Greg called out, "Tim, can we have that parcel please?"

The gate guard left the hut and passed Greg a large box. He was smiling and Hannah wondered why.

"There you go boss" the guard said, and retreated to his hut.

Greg and Hannah returned to the house where Greg passed the box to her.

"It's a surprise for you," he said, "I ordered it with your other clothes but held it back."

Hannah opened the box and gasped. She removed a pair of running shoes, shorts, running top and a black and red track suit.

"I take it I'm going for a jog?" she asked.

"Jog? No, a bit of a run. I need to see how physically fit you are. Tomorrow is a day off, Wednesday we'll be climbing Snowdon. In the evenings, a run, followed by weapons training. Add to that some basic concealment training, and we should be good to go. But first, a meal I think. I'm bloody starving!"

"If I'm going to be trained, Greg" said Hannah, "I'm going to cook you a meal this evening. Lamb Kleftiko. We need to pop to the supermarket for a few ingredients, but that won't take long. Let's go to the pub for lunch? It will be nice to see Tracey again. And I can show off my dress."

Greg took her in his arms.

"Hannah, if you go out looking that gorgeous, there'll be riots in the shops!"

Hannah beamed with pride,

"Maybe," she replied, "But they'll soon see that there is only one man for me." And with that, she kissed him, hard and urgently. It felt good, to both of them.

Greg threw a couple of shopping bags into the boot of the MG and they set off, roof down, enjoying their own company as well as the sunny day. Tracey greeted them with hugs, and the locals looked on with admiration as Hannah twirled her dress. Lunch was a simple Ploughman's, accompanied by lemon and lime. No alcohol, as Greg did not drink and drive. Then they drove into Caernarfon and bought the ingredients Hannah needed. A large shoulder of lamb was joined in the basket by Sugardrop tomatoes, onions, potatoes and a bottle of Domaine Trouillet Chardonnay. As they strolled among the aisles, Greg saw many men casting admiring glances at Hannah and felt a mix of pride and, to some small degree, jealousy. Pride overruled though and they left, hand in hand. As ever, Greg was cautious and carried out his anti-surveillance. Nothing stood out. They drove home and Greg left Hannah in the kitchen, preparing the evening meal. He sat on the decking and smoked. His mind wandered, to the run later, to how he would approach the weapons training and to the visit to London, the next day. Sav was with Hannah, no doubt looking for the occasional scrap. Hannah, however, knew not to give him cooked lamb bones and so contented herself with throwing the dog the jerky she had bought. Sav wolfed it down and his eyes implored her for more. She laughed,

"Sav, can't have you getting fat, mate. Enough for now."

The dog lay down by the door, as protective as he could be. Once the meal was in the slow cooker, Hannah joined Greg on the decking and shared a cigarette with him. The hammock seat gently swayed as they sat, in companionable silence, enjoying each other's company, like old friends.

Chapter 18

The General.

'Dickie' Gerrard-Wright sat at his desk. Jenny sat opposite him. She had related the details of her trip to Snowdonia and the General was not happy.

"We simply cannot have untrained personnel involved in anything like this, Jenny!" he said. "She'll need to undergo training in Hereford, just like you and Greg did. She could be a bloody liability in the field."

"Greg won't sanction it and, to be honest, we don't have the time, Sir." Jenny responded. "I realise the dangers, but Greg will provide basic training and, well, she'll be more background help, to be honest. I like her. She's got balls, put me in my place that's for sure!"

Dickie laughed, "I'd like to have seen that! Very well, run the plan by me again, then I'll evaluate the girl tomorrow."

Back in Snowdonia, Greg and Hannah changed into their running gear and set off. Once out of the gate, they turned right and jogged the mile to the main road. The road led through the village towards Caernarfon and Greg kept up a medium, steady pace. He glanced at Hannah but saw no sign that she was out of her depth. Once clear of the village, they turned left along a cycle track, past stables and fields of sheep and horses, running steadily. They saw few people, and none that Greg recognised. In spite of the apparent easing of tensions between him and Flaka, Greg was taking no chances, and had planned their route accordingly. For the most part, the journey was downhill and neither found it too difficult. They crossed the steam railway tracks and then hit another main road, past a large Tesco and, five miles after starting, arrived in the town centre, where Greg called a halt.

"Fancy a drink?" he asked her.

"Oh you bet!" Hannah laughed, "Water is overrated!"

The Castle pub was on The Maes and the pair went in, Greg ordering lime and sodas. Gwyndaf, the owner, looked them over.

"Don't see you much these days, Greg" he said, "Been taking your business elsewhere?"

Greg chuckled, "Not really mate, been a tad busy. This is Hannah, by the way." The two shook hands.

"I've heard a bit about you, young lady" Gwyndaf said, appraising Hannah. "Word travels fast in this area. Hope you are keeping Greg on a tight leash?" he chuckled, beckoning them to a quiet corner.

Gwyndaf had been in the Metropolitan Police for many years, ending up in Special Branch. His network of contacts remained as good today as ever before. He leaned towards them and said, in a conspiratorial tone,

"Spot of bother, I believe?" Neither replied. He continued, "Like I say, no secrets around here. Any help you need, just say, ok?"

Greg nodded, "Thanks Gwyndaf, always good to know."

Gwyndaf nodded, "And how is the lovely Ms Carpenter? I hear she's bought a BMW. Strange girl that, needs a good man, if you know what I mean!"

It was Hannah's turn to laugh.

"I'd feel very sorry for him, Gwyndaf" she said, "She's a ball breaker, that one!" Gwyndaf roared with laughter, his huge frame shaking.

"Oh Hannah, I like you! I think young Greg here has met his match, too!" They chatted for a few minutes before Greg announced they would be returning home.

"Safe home you two" Gwyndaf said, "And don't forget my invite!" The pair left the pub laughing and set off back the way they had come. It was very different this time as most of the journey was uphill, and Greg kept up a steady pace. Hannah again surprised him by showing no signs of tiredness, occasionally drinking from her water bottle, but pacing herself so that she did not run out too soon. As they got near the house, Greg suddenly put a spurt on and sprinted for the gate, beating Hannah by a few seconds. They laughed as they waited for Tim to open the gate.

"That's cheating!" Hannah said, "Race you to the front door! And was off. Greg overtook her and sprinted along the winding driveway. He looked behind him but of Hannah, there was no sight. As he approached the last curve in the road, he saw Hannah standing by the door of the house.

"How the...?" he panted.

"Well, you took the road, I simply cut across the field. Two can cheat, you know!"

They almost fell into the house, laughing. Sav greeted them fondly and the smell of oregano, cooking with the lamb, hit their noses. Greg sniffed,

"Wow, that smells good. Right, time for a shower, a change and then dinner?" Hannah nodded, "Me first please." And dived into the bathroom. Greg went into the kitchen and fed Sav. Half an hour later, Hannah emerged, this time in the tracksuit and smiled at him.

"You next, smelly!" she said, and ducked out of the room, Sav trotting behind her. She sat in the conservatory, awaiting Greg's return. Greg showered and also changed into his tracksuit. They now matched and Hannah liked that. They sat and ate dinner before going outside and having a cigarette. It was probably his only vice. Smoking just a few a day helped him to unwind. Hannah felt the same. When they had finished, Greg led the way into the cellar. Hannah looked around. It seemed small and she could not see what they would be doing by way of training down here. Each wall was twenty feet long and ten feet high. Along one side were gun cabinets, securely locked, and bolted to the wall. At the far end was a panelled wall which Greg walked towards. He touched the middle and the wall folded back, revealing a room roughly one hundred feet long. The only lights were at the far end, and they lit a series of targets on wires. Hannah gasped.

"Wow! Who built this?"

Greg explained that, during World War Two, a series of underground bunkers were built all across the UK. They would contain weapons and ammunition to enable the population to strike back in the event of invasion.

"Even the estate agent didn't know it was here" Greg explained. "Dickie did, and pointed me in the right direction. It's perfect for weapons training."

He strode towards a cabinet and unlocked it. Taking out a pistol, he checked the magazine was empty and then cocked the weapon to ensure there was not a round in the breech. Satisfied, he handed it to Hannah.

"This, Hannah, is a Browning Hi Power, 9mm pistol. It's an excellent weapon. It's probably the most used pistol in history. It weighs just under a kilo, holds thirteen rounds in the magazine and is effective up to fifty metres. It has stopping power. If it has a fault at all, the pistol tends to bite the web of the hand, between the thumb and the forefinger. You'll get used to it. The Hi Power is the first pistol I ever fired and I was impressed. I still am."

Greg then showed her how to load the magazine, but he only put ten rounds in.

"We don't keep the magazines loaded. That weakens the spring. Also, the magazine 'feed lips', see here? They tend to degrade, so I never fill the magazine up. Now, here's how to load." He showed her and then turned towards the targets.

"Put those ear defenders on" he instructed, placing his own over his ears. He then simply held out his right arm, aimed, and fired at a target. The noise was deafening, even through the ear protection. When he'd finished, he placed the pistol on a table by his side, magazine ejected.

Greg pressed a button and his target slid effortlessly towards him. He sighed.

"Bugger!" he said, "Out of practice."

Hannah gazed at the holes, smack in the centre of the paper target. One, however, was outside the bull. Greg pointed to it.

"First round. I jerked the trigger. Ok, your turn."

He handed Hannah ten rounds of 9mm ammunition and the magazine. She loaded the magazine as she had been shown, then slid it into the base of the pistol grip. Surprisingly, she checked the safety was on. Greg smiled. 'Quick learner' he thought. Pointing to the left target, he told Hannah to cock the weapon and fire, in her own time. Hannah held the pistol two handed, feet apart, just as she'd seen on films. She squinted along the barrel and started firing. Greg remained silent until she had finished, then he buzzed the target back towards them.

"FUCK!" he exclaimed! "Where did you learn to shoot?" The target had ten holes within the bull and Greg was mega impressed.

"This is my first time" Hannah said, feeling incredibly proud. Greg handed her ten more rounds which she loaded into the magazine. This time was target two, second from the left. Again, ten bulls. Greg carried this out five times and Hannah didn't miss once. He beamed with pride.

"Hannah, if Flaka saw that he'd run a fecking mile! Bloody well done. I'm so proud of you. Welcome to the TEAM!" and with that he kissed her. The smell of cordite was strong in the cellar and so they went back upstairs, but not before checking the pistol. Greg tucked it into his belt.

"I'll show you cleaning next. After every time of use, we always clean. I'm happy Hannah, you never cease to surprise me." He shook his head and led the way. Once upstairs, Greg sat in the conservatory and stripped the pistol. Using a pull through and a piece of 4 x 2 cloth material, he oiled the rag and pulled it through the barrel. He then oiled every part and left it on the coffee table.

"One question, Hannah, are firearms dangerous?"

Hannah considered her answer.

"Well, yes, but only when a human has hold of one. I mean, that pistol won't hurt anyone where it is, but if someone picked it up, put it back together and loaded it, then, yes, it's dangerous."

Greg put his arm around her.

"Spot on." He said. He then reassembled the pistol and placed it in the small of his back.

"You will have your own personal weapon, but not this. You'll have a Walther PPK, the one you took the mick out of the other day. There's a reason for that. If you ever have the need to use it, it'll be up close and personal. Final resort, if you like. I want you prolific in that weapon. Firing at the standstill is one thing, but I'll get you firing from all angles."

"Now then, I think you need to see the Bunkhouse. The guys live there when on campus, so it might be a bit smelly. But there's something else there that I'd like to show you." He stood and they left the house, Sav trotting behind. When they arrived at the Bunkhouse, Greg opened the door.

"The other night, when we came in, you missed something. Not surprising, you were distracted by the arm wrestling." He walked to the end of the room and drew back a huge curtain. Beyond was a gymnasium. Whilst small, it had all the equipment needed to keep the guys fit and occupy their minds. Along the left-hand wall were a cycle machine, a power rack, a mini trampoline and a rowing machine. Along the opposite side were a dip station, a pull up bar, a bench press and sets of dumbbells. As he had predicted, the smell of sweat pervaded their nostrils. Sav had stayed at the door, obviously not a fan of sweat. Hannah walked around, touching different equipment. She looked at Greg,

"I like it, but I've never used any of this. Will you teach me?"

"Of course. We start tomorrow night. Harry will be here with an exercise programme he's designed just for you. In the far corner is a punch bag. By way of incentive, we're putting a photo of Flaka on it. Should encourage us both to beat the crap out of it!" he laughed. Hannah joined him.

"Greg, this is, well, just amazing. I don't know what to say, I really don't. You are taking such a chance with me. I can't thank you enough."

Greg smiled.

"Hannah, believe me. I'm putting my whole faith in you. I don't do that very often. The thing is, I know my faith is justified. Totally. And, by way of celebrating, I think we deserve a glass of wine."

That night, when they went to bed, Hannah and Greg held each other close. There seemed to be an unspoken agreement that nothing else would happen, just yet. They lay in the darkness, not speaking until they both drifted off to sleep. Tomorrow would be a busy day but at least they would be together.

Chapter 19.

Officer Down.

Dardan Flaka paced around his office. Neither his, nor McReanor's, enquiries had unearthed any information about DooM, Drugs out of Manchester. The mules he had used were adamant that the group were dangerous. No firearms had been involved, just extremely good tactics. They tried to describe their attackers but, other than black trousers and jumpers, accompanied with full face balaclava's, nothing useful emerged. Flaka was not just furious, he was puzzled. Messages to his fellow drugs gang leaders had yielded nothing. They had not been targeted so really didn't care. Dardan was also worried. Undue attention was being paid to him by the media, especially since the warehouse debacle. His associates had warned the reporters off but that wouldn't last for ever. The Manchester Evening News had the headline 'Doom! Drugs out of Manchester group play vigilante' They cited Flaka's warehouse with the speculation that DooM had been involved. The police refused to comment. Flaka stood in front of Granit, whose face was healing slowly. Albana stood nearby, waiting for the explosion of anger from her father. Luckily, it failed to materialise. Dardan was calm, which, if his enemies saw it, was a very dangerous sign.

"So" he said, more to himself than to anyone else, "nothing about this vigilante group DooM? Okay, we carry on as normal. Change the mules, change the routes. Arm the mules if necessary. I have lost, no, money was STOLEN from me. £100,000! This cannot go unpunished. Someone is giving information. Granit, you and Ismet will now find out who. Bring them to me!"

Granit nodded.

"My pleasure Boss!" he said, standing. "I am right on this." He left the room and Albana sighed with relief. Tonight she was seeing Salim again but not at her house. At his. She had no idea that the house was bugged. Had she known; she would have ripped the walls apart.

Davey McReanor was also worried. Flaka had given him an ultimatum, find the grasses or else! There was not a lot Davey could do whilst on duty but, off duty, he trawled the streets, talking to his contacts but getting nowhere. Nobody had heard of DooM. The usual suspects had been questioned but, yet again, nothing. Davey feared they were looking in the wrong place. He suspected that Greg Angel was involved but surveillance reports suggested Angel had a perfect alibi. But the thought still nagged at him. He applied for seven days leave, which was granted immediately. His senior officers were glad to be rid of him, if just for a week. That night, Davey visited a young prostitute. She looked fourteen but was, in fact, over thirty. As he approached the bed where she lay, naked and trembling, McReanor failed to hear the footsteps approaching the door. At once, it was kicked open, and one man burst in. Dressed all in black and with a full-face balaclava, he fired two rounds into Davey's head. The girl didn't scream, the drugs had dulled her senses. Rather, she stood, dressed quickly, and left with the attacker. Money changed hands and she disappeared into the night. No one would ever know she was there. The shooter left the building and walked away, leaving the weapon behind.

This would be a problem to the police. Despite McReanor being a complete arsehole, he was still a copper. The shooter knew this, and smiled.

The next morning, Greg woke Hannah at 5 am. She looked at him groggily,

"What? It's still dark!"

Greg chuckled,

"And we have a long drive ahead of us. I've got coffee on, Sav is being looked after by the guards, and we are on the road!"

Hannah shook her hair,

"Can I at least get dressed?" she said.

"Oh, well, if you have to!" Greg replied, watching as this vision stepped out of the bed. "The General will be happy to see you either way." On his way out of the bedroom, he blew her a kiss. That simple action touched her heart. Hannah dressed in jeans and a white t shirt and ran to the bathroom. She thought back. Relationships in her life had, so far, been few and far between, but she could not remember being so content. She sighed,

'And how long did they last?' she thought. Then reality set in and she realised that, for some insane reason, she was in deep. Once in the kitchen, she drank a black coffee and watched as Greg prepared the MG. He checked oil, water, tyres, everything in fact. Then she joined him.

"Ready Boss?" she said, an intimate smile on her face.

"Bring a book sweetheart" Greg replied, and then cursed. "I'm sorry, I shouldn't have called you that!" he muttered.

Hannah looked him in the eyes.

"Why not?" she asked.

Greg floundered,

"Well, you might not have liked it." He replied, embarrassed.

Hannah took his hands and placed them on her shoulders.,

"Oh Greg," she whispered to him, "You have so much to learn!"

Greg moved away and went back into the house, his mind in turmoil. Hannah came into the room and the atmosphere was tense for a while. Then Greg announced they should leave. Hannah sat next to him as they negotiated their way to the A55 where Greg floored the accelerator. The rumble of the exhaust filled their ears and Hannah read her book. Then she suddenly stopped.

"Greg" she said, "I was given a book whilst I sat begging" she sighed, the memory still raw, "A book by Stephen Leather, about a guy called Spider Shepherd. A book about 'Black ops'. Is that what I'm involved in now?"

Greg smiled at her, trying to be reassuring.

"Hannah. Can I just say that, once you meet The General, everything will, I hope, become clear? Yes, Stephen Leathers books are excellent. Maybe read one of Harry's books?"

Hannah looked at him aghast.

"Harry? As in our Harry?" she asked.

"Oh feck!" Greg said, "I thought you'd noticed his books on my bookshelf. Yes, Harry is a writer. Very accomplished too. Non-fiction only is our Harry. Total fact. You can believe every word he writes. Harry doesn't do fiction. Trust me, he's a man of hidden depths and talents."

Hannah took that in. Then a question formed in her mind and she risked asking it.

"And you? Have you written any books?"

Greg roared with laughter.

"Sweetheart" he answered, "I find it hard to write an email!"

They settled into the journey until Jenny called.

"Hi Greg and his better half!" both laughed, "I've booked you into the Union Jack Club, hope it suits! Oh, and you have an old friend at Empire House. I take it you remember the way?" followed by a chuckle. It was Hannah who replied.

"His better half here, Jenny. Many thanks. I guess the old guy can still remember?"

Greg chuckled, "The 'old guy is still compos mentis you know! Yes, Jenny, I remember, and thanks. Now, would you two like to have dinner this evening without the encumbrance of a pensioner?"

Jenny roared with laughter,

"But, then, who would pay?" she responded, before quickly cutting the connection. Greg and Hannah looked at each other and laughed.

"She's actually quite nice" Hannah said. "Maybe Harry would like to write my life story?" although she was joking. Greg nodded,

"Yes. I'd like to read it."

Hannah shook her head vigorously,

"In that case, NO!" she said. Greg looked at her and replied,

"Why? In case it puts me off you? Hannah, trust me, nothing could distract me from you. Nothing. Hannah, I'll be forty-five on Christmas day. You are only twenty-four. Questions will be asked."

Hannah burst out laughing.

"Really? By whom? Not by the Team. They realise that we are meant to be together. Tracey said so. And she's perceptive. What about Gwyndaf? An 'invite'? Did you miss that? I almost did. Everyone knows apart from us two. Time to get real, I think?"

The Welcome Break Services were approaching fast and Greg directed the MG off the motorway. After parking, he took Hannah in his arms and held her tight. They remained silent until Greg reminded them of their appointment. Hannah said one more thing before they left.

"And even Jenny, what did she say? 'Greg and his better half?' We even have her blessing. Now then, let's go see your General. I'm looking forward to this. If he's half the man I think he is, then he's one hell of a guy!"

Chapter 20.

Gore Downey

D.I 'Gore' Downey stood looking down at McReanor's body. It lay face down on a filthy mattress, blood drying around the wounds. Gore's meeting with the Chief Constable had been awkward, to say the least.

"McReanor was an arsehole Downey! But he was still a cop. I want the bastard who shot him, and soon!"

Gore had nodded in agreement. Cop killers were the worst kind in his book, no matter the victim. Sergeant Paddy Burrows, Gore's sidekick, stood by the door.

"The list of suspects is a long one, Gore" he said, trying to avert his eyes from the lifeless body. Gore nodded.

"Maybe, but I want each and every one found, interviewed and grilled. Who is the chief suspect?"

Burrows looked at his boss.

"Dardan Flaka," he said, "And if we're going to drag him in, I'm in the squad that arrest him!"

Gore chuckled, "You and me both Paddy, you and me both. I want a crack at that fat bastard Granit. I've heard he got a kicking at the hands of some street tough recently. I'd like to hear about it from the arses mouth!"

Burrows chuckled.

"Hardly a street tough, Guv. Sounds like the guy was an expert in street fighting. Some bouncers saw it happen and said they'd not go near the guy if he kicked off. Rescued some homeless girl too. Not been seen again. Mind, I heard that McReanor was making enquiries about it. I'll check the computer. This 'hero' may even be a suspect?"

"Maybe Paddy, maybe. My money is on Flaka, although he'll have paid someone. That scumbag won't get his own hands dirty." Gore's Northern Irish accent came to the fore at moments like this. If asked to describe himself, Downey might have said he had a penchant for church music, raw meat and hookers! The last one with a wry smile. He has specific enemies, both within the police and criminal fraternity. Mainly due to his diligence in catching crooks. Gore did not admit defeat, something that made him a formidable foe, either back in Belfast or in Manchester. He always checked under his car before getting into it. He told his children it was in case a cat had crawled under, but, as he'd survived two murder attempts, he took no chances.

Gore turned away,

"Let's go Paddy. Work to do." They set off in Gore's car. When they arrived at Central Station, Gore went up to report to the Chief Constable. Gore treated everybody with respect until they treated him otherwise. The Chief held Gore in high regard but he was under pressure. The explosion and fire in Birkenhead were being linked to a thug mafia boss in his area and the Home Office wanted answers. Strangely, he had heard on his grapevine that there was a ban on information about any possible suspects. One person, was Greg Angel. Gore did not know him but, if he had committed a crime, Gore would have him. No matter any protection the government might offer. The briefing went as expected, no clues, no immediate suspects. Gore offered his opinion.

"Sir" he started, "McReanor was looking for intel on a guy who battered two of Flaka's thugs. Burrows has found out who this guy is. Greg Angel. We've tried to get intel on him but we're being blocked, and I don't fucking like that!"

The Chief looked hard at his Inspector.

"Then we'll have to unblock it! Do you have his address etc?"

Gore nodded,

"Aye, so we do. Maybe a visit?"

The Chief nodded.

"Yes, but notify the local cops. Where does he live?"

"Snowdonia, Sir" Gore smiled, seeing his boss blanche at the possible overtime. "Sure, don't worry Sir, I'm due a day off, and I rather fancy climbing Snowdon. No charge, Sir!"

The Chief smiled.

"Least we can do is pay your hotel, Gore! Put in a claim for, erm, mileage, eh?"

Gore left the office and met Paddy in the corridor.

"Like Wales do you, Paddy?" he asked, a smirk on his face.

"Fucking hate the place, Boss" Burrows replied, "But I guess I'm going there?"

"Tomorrow, Paddy. Bring your passport and get inoculated!"

As Greg approached London, Hannah asked a question.

"Greg" she started, "I don't want to upset you, but, well, what was Miriam like?"

He thought for a moment before replying.

"Miriam was a character. Loved by all. Respected. And a great cop. She had heart and compassion. One night, when we'd only been partnered for a few days, we got called to a domestic. I was still a newbie and had to follow her lead. But she gave me the chance to prove my worth. When we arrived, the 'lady' of the house opened the door and hurled abuse at us and everyone else. I went in first and Miriam finally got out of the woman that her husband was upstairs with a knife and he'd threatened her. I told

Miriam to keep the woman downstairs and made my way up. Miriam, called to me, 'Safe, Greg, safe, ok?' I carried on and, at the top of the stairs, in the larger bedroom, was a man, armed with a huge carving knife. He screamed at me to stay away but I went in. There was an old battered wicker chair to one side and I sat in it. The guy stayed where he was. He asked if I was going to arrest him. I countered with asking him how long he'd been married. 'Twenty years' he replied. I chuckled, 'In that case my friend, you deserve a fucking medal! She pissed me off after two minutes!'. He actually smiled. He then put the knife down and sat on the bed. 'Jaysus, peeler' he said, 'but you're a funny cop. Why didn't ye shoot me?' 'What for?' I asked, 'being married for twenty years?' We both laughed and I held out my hand for the knife. He had an address he could go to, so we took him there. No further police action. Unknown to me, Miriam had been outside, ready to intervene. The guy came to the station next morning and thanked me, in front of Inspector Murphy, for keeping the situation under control. I often wonder what happened to him. Inspector Murphy and I didn't get on. To him I was a smartarse Brit who should fuck off back to England."

Hannah chuckled.

"Compassion? I think you've got it too Greg" she said.

Greg nodded, then overtook a slow-moving car, flooring the accelerator.

"Compassion didn't stop Miriam being murdered!" Then he calmed. "Sorry" he whispered.

Hannah looked concerned.

"Greg" she said, "Were the killers ever caught?"

"No. They are still at large. Two are so-called Community workers. One is a local councillor and one is a politician. No justice, yet!"

"Are you thinking of going after them?" she said.

"Not yet, Hannah. But one day. At least, until I met you. Maybe not now. The TEAM could deal with them but it would be without the General's sanction, which would make me a criminal, a murderer. I've you to think about now."

Hannah touched his hand tenderly.

"If you do, I'm going with you, okay?"

Greg blinked away a tear.

"Deal," he replied, softly, "Deal". Problem was, he didn't mean it.

The motorway ended and Greg was forced to slow down. His car drew admiring glances as they threaded their way into central London.

As they entered Central London, Greg aimed for Camden Town. His final destination was Regents Park Barracks, in Albany Street. He had spent some time there on a course, years ago. He described the surrounding areas to Hannah, and mentioned the barracks.

"When the SAS stormed the Iranian Embassy, they trained in this barracks." He said. Hannah asked the obvious question,

"Were you on that?"

He laughed, "No sweetheart, but I hear that some 40,000 were!"

He signalled left before the entrance and turned in, slowly, hands in full view. Immediately two soldiers, armed with SA 80 rifles, checked him out. He provided identity and explained who they were to see. The guards saluted, which tickled Hannah. Greg drove in, swung left then immediately right. Straight on was an imposing single storey building.

"Empire House" Greg said. "My love, we have arrived. I hope the General has arranged lunch; I'm starving!" Hannah agreed.

They exited the car and were met by a Sergeant Major.

"Mr Angel" he said, whilst standing at attention. "The General is expecting you. And Ms Carpenter is due soon, I believe."

"I'm a civvy now, Ted" Greg said, shaking the Sarn't Major's hand. "let's cut the crap, eh?"

The non-commissioned Warrant Officer smiled.

"Feck but you don't change!" he said, hugging Greg warmly. "And you must be Hannah? Pleasure to meet you."

Hannah shook the outstretched paw, rather like that of a huge bear. Greg did the introductions.

"Ted is the Sergeant Major of this place. Ex Black Watch. The hardest man in the British Army, but also the nicest."

Ted led them into the building and towards the back. Greg remembered this as being the Officer's Mess, back in the day. One place he never frequented. At the end of a corridor sat a desk, and, behind it, was a stunning blonde Corporal, in her day dress uniform. She smiled,

"Please go straight in" she said.

Ted left the pair there. Greg knocked loudly,

"Come in Greg, for God's sake!" a deep resonant voice called.

They entered and Greg was amazed to see the General in full uniform. The officer stood and walked to their side of the desk.

"Greg dear boy. Good to see you. And you must be the lady who has captivated his heart?"

He held out his hand and Hannah stopped herself from curtseying.

"Good to see you too, Sir" Greg managed.

"Sir? Come, come Greg, we've known each other long enough for you to call me Dickie!" and retreated behind his desk. Hannah thought to be cheeky,

"Can I call you Dickie too, Sir?" she asked, eyes twinkling.

The General roared with laughter,

"My dear lady" he said, "You may call me whatever you like, as long as it is often! Sue, my wife, will be here soon, Greg. You haven't been in touch as much as she would like you know!"

Greg and Hannah sat in the plush chairs offered to them.

"I apologise, Sir, I mean, Dickie" he said, "Been a tad busy."

Dickie looked at Hannah,

"We go way back Hannah" he said, "Has Greg told you about.."

Greg interrupted,

"No Sir, I haven't. Have you ordered lunch? We're rather hungry."

Dickie nodded and appreciated Greg's reticence.

"Better than that, old boy, lunch at the White House Hotel, just down the road. Jenny will join us there, erm, after our chat."

Hannah was fascinated.

"I'm keen to hear everything General" she said.

Dickie coughed.

"Maybe, young lady, maybe. I need to introduce myself properly though. I'm retired from the army but still work for the security of this great country of ours. So does Greg and his TEAM. A fine bunch, if I may say so too, Greg. My official title is Director of Military Intelligence. I run, er, operations, on behalf of the government. We are sort of official and young Greg here is a vital cog in our wheel. Not used much but when he is, it's a matter of national security. By the way, you are bound by the Official Secrets Act. Anything you hear in this room is a secret. Divulging that to anyone, at any time, will result in your imprisonment. I hope we understand each other?"

Hannah nodded, stunned. This was a totally different world to her, but she trusted Greg and his associates implicitly. The General continued,

"Greg and the TEAM, 'help' us out occasionally, with matters that cannot be made public. In return, we 'help' Greg out with equipment etc. Greg has helped me out on several occasions, in one, when he was in the army, he saved my life. For which Sue is eternally grateful."

Hannah looked at Greg who appeared embarrassed. She held him in high regard anyway but this? Saving the life of a Senior Officer? Wow. She was blown away. Greg sought to diffuse the situation,

"Right place, right time, Sir" he said, hoping the conversation would move on rapidly. The General humphed,

"Quite so, Greg, quite so. Anyway, here in RPB as we call it, we coordinate operations against terrorists. Your Mr Flaka being one."

Now, Hannah was totally amazed. She knew Flaka was a bad egg, but a terrorist? Just how lucky had she been to meet Greg? She thought. Dickie noted her expression.

"Yes, my dear, Flaka is one very bad person. His contacts with Muslim extremists are unbelievable. One nasty bastard, if you'll excuse my French" he smiled, indulgently. Hannah thanked him.

"Sir," she said, quietly, "I know how grateful I am to Greg. But this? I will help in any way I can."

Greg nodded and held her hand.

"Dickie" he said, smiling, "This lady can shoot a peanut off a rhino's, erm, well, you get the drift!"

Dickie laughed,

"Of course." They chatted about events since Greg had met Hannah, and Dickie was even more impressed with the man who sat, quietly, before him. 'Hidden depths', he thought. Just then there was a rap on the door. Ted, the Sergeant Major, entered.

"Your good lady has arrived, Sir" he said, and Sue swept into the room. Ignoring her husband, she made a bee line for Greg.

"Greg!" she gushed, "Naughty boy, ignoring me!" Then her eyes met Hannah's. "But I see why. My dear, I am Sue, the long-suffering husband of the reprobate sat there. My, Greg" she continued, "At long last, you have extremely good taste!"

Hannah stood looking at Sue. The lady before her was slim, immaculately turned out and, for a woman who must have been in her late sixties, totally gorgeous.

"Thank you, Sue" she managed. "It's wonderful to meet you. Greg has told me nothing about you, yet!" She smiled but glared at Greg, who simply smiled.

"Sue, may I introduce you to Hannah."

Sue smiled back,

"Nothing to worry about Hannah. Just that Greg is our dearest friend. My daughters adore him but, luckily, they're both married. Get him to tell you about the shopping trip! It's hilarious. Now then Dickie, can we eat? And I take it the government are paying?"

Dickie smiled and ushered them outside. An army mini bus was waiting, a Royal Logistics Corps driver at the door. They climbed aboard and set off; Hannah still impressed at being saluted!

Two minutes later, they entered the hotel where a flunky showed them to a table, set in the corner. Greg took a seat facing the exit, old habits dying hard. Sue started the conversation,

"Are you ok for a glass of wine Greg?" she enquired, not looking at Hannah. Greg nodded,

"Yes, Sue" he said, "I'm okay now"

Hannah looked the question at him and he realised he had to tell her.

"Hannah. When I came back to the mainland, after, after Miriam, I sought refuge in the bottle. Vodka mainly. That's why I never touch it now. I got arrested a couple of times and Sue and Dickie bailed me out. Pulled strings, that sort of thing. Then I came to my senses and only drink occasionally now. I'm sorry. I sound so fecking feeble!"

His eyes went to the ceiling as he composed himself. Hannah touched his hand tenderly.

"I understand Greg, I really do."

Sue looked at her husband. The exchanged look said it all. Greg was in love. So was Hannah. Wonders will never cease. She decided to break the atmosphere.

"Now then Greg, I know you hate lobster, but I like it. I take it you'll have your usual steak, well done?"

Greg thanked her and Hannah ordered the same. They exchanged glances, as did Sue and Dickie. This was going to be a delicate phase of Greg's life, and Dickie needed to be on his best mettle.

The meal passed peacefully after that. Greg thought that things had been ruined by his admission. Luckily, he was wrong. Jenny hadn't arrived for lunch but no comment was made by anyone. Greg and Hannah bade Sue a fond farewell. In the afternoon, Dickie showed Greg and Hannah the facilities at the barracks. Hannah was impressed. They also discussed Flaka and Dickie gave Greg carte blanche to take what action he thought necessary, but with a word of caution.

"Jenny couldn't make lunch. With good reason, it appears. There's a Detective Inspector. Gordon Downey. He's after whoever set the warehouse alight. Watch him. He's keen and he's bloody good. I can help, but only to a certain extent. One of his Sergeants, a Davey McReanor, was killed yesterday."

Greg and Hannah looked at each other in surprise.

"Does he suspect me?" Greg said.

"Well, let's say you are on the list. Expect a visit. He's bloody tenacious. Tread carefully. Alibi sorted?"

"None needed, as I have no idea when this McReanor was killed." Greg responded.

"Good. That's that then. Time to wrap things up. I'll let Jenny fill you in on the plan. It seems this Inspector is planning to visit you tomorrow in Wales. But, as you are staying here tonight, he'll be unlucky, eh?" Dickie laughed. "Have a lovely evening both. Speak soon." With that the three shook hands and left the Officers Mess.

Greg drove Hannah to the Union Jack Club in Waterloo. She gazed at the modern façade and sighed with joy when the entered the large reception. Within minutes, they were in a lift, heading for their room. Greg had packed a small bag of essentials but no change of clothes for Hannah. He explained that they could buy anything she needed and, he told her, she would need a mobile phone. They threw the bag on the king size bed and left the room again. Hannah linked her arm into Greg's.

"This place is gorgeous!" she said. "Not like I expected." Greg agreed. It was his first time staying there as well, but now, mid-afternoon, there was some serious shopping to be done. They hit Oxford Street, Greg careful to keep himself between Hannah and anyone else, constantly on the alert. First they bought Hannah a leather jacket, matching Greg's. Then more jeans, trainers and a couple of dresses. Then they spotted a phone shop and they entered. The Sales Assistant asked what they were looking for and Greg looked at Hannah. But she looked perplexed.

"Tell you what, Hannah" Greg said, "My phone is the Landrover Explorer. Excellent phone and comes with a second battery for when off exploring the countryside. How about that?"

Hannah looked at Greg's phone and agreed. Greg had the phone put onto Vodafone, the same as his. Harry would make a few alterations to it later. The Assistant seemed pleased to find such quick customers and, within half an hour, the pair left. Greg suggested Hannah get a shoulder bag and they went into a large shop, on Piccadilly. Hannah chose a leather bag, in a soft black colour and Greg insisted she put it on, but over her shoulder and across her chest.

"Bag snatchers won't normally try to take it if it's too difficult to get off" he said. Hannah placed her phone inside and smiled.

"I'll need a purse, too" she said, and the young female assistant hurried away, returning with a selection. A soft black leather purse was agreed upon. Greg paid and they returned, at a leisurely pace, armed with multiple shopping bags, to the hotel. Greg had parked the MG in one of the few spaces in the basement car park and the pair put most of the shopping in the boot. Hannah kept two bags, however.

"Clothes for this evening" she explained. Once in the lift, heading up to their room, Hannah hugged Greg.

"You really are an Angel, you know!" she said, contentment showing in her smile. Greg stayed quiet. To him, he was just acting as any normal human should do. He felt he was doing nothing special, but it was nice to be appreciated.

They arrived at their room and Greg ordered coffee to be

sent up. Hannah went into the shower. The room was no smoking and so he sat on the balcony, cigarette in hand, musing. This had been some day! The news that a police Inspector was interested in him was bad news. The TEAM thrived on secrecy, which must be kept. He decided to talk to Harry later, but, in the meantime, he telephoned the gate guard to warn them of the impending visit. That done, he took his turn in the shower but had no change of clothes. So, jeans, t shirt and leather jacket it was. Hannah emerged from the bathroom dressed in a black skirt, pale pink blouse and shoes with quite high heels. Greg whistled.

"As ever, young lady" he said, "Stunning."

She smiled and bowed.

Leaving the Club, Greg hailed a Black Cab, he distrusted Uber. They climbed in and the Cockney driver asked,

"Where to Guv?"

Greg sat forward, "Greek Street, please. Any recommendations on a good restaurant there? Not seafood though."

Greg was well aware that all Black Cab drivers knew everything there was to know about London. They had to complete 'The Knowledge' a gruelling set of challenges. There are some 25,000 streets in London and cabbies must know every one before becoming a fully-fledged taxi driver in the Capital.

The Knowledge was introduced way back in 1865 and still runs today. Greg appreciated these drivers. The cabbie thought for a moment,

"Do you like Greek food Guv?" he asked. Greg and Hannah nodded.

"Perfick, my son" the driver said, "Suvlaki House it is then. Great food, and, for a young couple like you two, very romantic."

Greg laughed,

"Thanks mate, much obliged." And sat back next to Hannah. She whispered,

"See? Even a taxi driver sees us as a couple." Greg nodded and kissed her lightly. A few minutes later, the cab pulled up outside the restaurant.

"A fiver Guv" the driver said, and was amazed when Greg gave him a twenty and said,

"Keep the change. Have a good evening." And the pair walked off. The driver looked after them and muttered,

"Stone the facking crows! What a diamond geezer. "

Greg and Hannah entered the restaurant, tastefully decorated in the Mediterranean Blue the Greeks favoured. The Head waiter, dressed immaculately in black trousers and crisp white shirt, greeted them. Greg asked for a private table for two and they were shown to the rear of the open plan room. Once seated,

Greg asked for Retsina, preferably Kourtakis.

The Head waiter smiled.

"Excellent choice Sir. And for the lady?"

Hannah said she'd try the same. Greg smiled as they sat opposite each other, Greg facing the door. He'd already identified the possible exits, old habits.

"How do you know about Greek wines?" Hannah asked him. He explained that he had holidayed in Greece many times. It was a country he loved.

"I went on a tour of the Kourtakis factory once. It was amazing. Such a kind, lovely, helpful people. I even met an old guy who had been in the resistance during WW2. He paddled his boat from the back, using one oar. Not one word of English did he speak, so I learned Greek to hear his tale. Fascinating man. Vasili, his Granddaughter, ran the hotel I stayed in. Happy times. I'll take you on holiday there if you wish?"

Hannah said it would be great. Little did the pair know that, their visit to Halkidiki, would not be a holiday.

When the wine arrived, Greg was pleased to note it was unopened. The Head Waiter introduced himself,

"Sir, I am Sasha. Tonight, I am at your service. Here is the Retsina you requested, and, may I say that, because of your impeccable taste, this is on the house!"

Sasha proceeded to uncork the bottle, it's yellow label

glinting in the light of the candle on the table, and poured Greg a small sample. Greg sniffed and then tasted.

"Perfect, thank you Sasha." who then poured two glasses of the golden liquid. Greg picked his glass up and said,

"Yamas, Sasha." The waiter smiled, "Yamas" he replied. The menu was placed before them and Sasha retreated, speaking in Greek to his staff. Greg pretended to not know what was being said but Hannah was keen to know. He took one of her hands and said,

"He told his staff that the young couple are experts on Greece and to make the meal we order, the finest they ever have. I like him."

They studied the menu and then ordered. For starters, Greg ordered Vine leaves with pine nuts and currants. Hannah licked her lips,

"Sounds heavenly!" she announced, causing Sasha to grin widely. When the subject of main course arose, Hannah pleaded,

"Please can we have Beef Stifado?" Sasha beamed once again. Tonight, for a change, he had real Greek lovers in his restaurant.

"Madam," he said, "Thank you. Beef Stifado it is."

Hannah chuckled, "I wonder if it's as good as Greg cooks?"

Sasha struggled for words so Greg helped him out,

"Sasha, I pretend to make the dish. However, I know that your chef will make the perfect Beef Stifado. Epharisto."

Left alone, the couple chatted. Mostly about the day shopping and what was needed. Greg told Hannah that Harry had organised her a Provisional Driving Licence and a bank account.

"But you don't know my surname!" Hannah exclaimed. Greg made a suggestion.

"Okay, I'll write down three surnames I think might belong to you. Then, you tell me the real one and we'll see if I've guessed correctly?"

Hannah agreed and Greg took a napkin and, after giving the matter some thought, wrote down three names.

"Now then Hannah" he said, "Over to you."

Hannah looked into his eyes, seeing nothing. She paused, before answering,

"It's 'Ball'. Not fun when you are Hannah Ball at school!"

Greg smiled.

"Damn!" he said, "I had you down for a Smith, Jones or Rogers! Oh well, can't be right all the time. I'll tell Harry tomorrow. He'll sort you out with a full set of documents. Mind, you can change your name, you know?"

Hannah said,

"But I've never driven a car in my life!"

"Ah, in that case, Tim will teach you. He's the best, trust me."

Hannah posed the question about name change. Greg told her,

"You can change your name, legally, by Deed Poll. Doesn't cost a lot and is fairly quick. What surname do you fancy?"

Hannah thought for a moment, taking a sip of Retsina,

"I'd like to be 'Hannah Angel'" she replied, simply, watching for Greg's reaction.

Greg paused before responding,

"I'd like that too." He said, a mile-wide smile across his face. He raised his glass in a toast,

"To Hannah Angel!" They clinked glasses and settled back to enjoy their evening.

The evening passed quickly. Sasha was very attentive and, when the couple looked up, all the chairs were on the tables and the staff stood by the bar. Greg was horrified.

"Oh my goodness, Sasha!" he cried, "I'm so sorry. We have detained you all." Sasha simply bowed and said,

"Sir, to see a couple so much in love is a pleasure. No problems, I promise."

Greg paid the bill on his card and added the ten percent service charge.

Then he shook hands with the waiters and the chef and handed each of them a ten-pound note.

"To thank you for all your service" he said in Greek. He continued, in the same tongue, "I thank you for a fantastic evening. "Each person smiled and thanked him. As the pair left the restaurant, Sasha called after them.

"Sir, a small gift." He then presented Greg with a bottle of Metaxa 12 Star, wrapped in the Greek flag. Greg was touched and shook the waiter's hand.

"Epharisto, Kirea!" he said. Once outside, Greg again hailed a cab and they went back to Waterloo and the hotel. Both felt well fed and extremely warm.

'Life just doesn't get better than this!' Greg thought. But it can get much worse, as they were about to discover.

When the couple arrived back at the Union Jack Club, Greg collected the key and they took the lift. Once in the room, they simply looked at each other. Knowing looks. Greg took her in his arms and kissed her, passionately. Then he undressed her and carried her to the bed, lying alongside her. No words were spoken. Hannah undressed him, in between kisses, and they lay on top of the duvet. Their love making was slow, and unhurried. To both, it felt fantastic. After, they lay gazing into each other's eyes, both unsure of the other's feelings. Eventually, Greg spoke.

"I love you Hannah" he said, simply. She responded, "I love

you too, Greg" And that was that. They slipped beneath the duvet and held each other tightly. During the night, they would make love twice more, each time seemingly more passionate.

Next morning, Greg held Hannah in his arms. He chuckled,

"If you say, not bad for an old guy, I'll smack your bare bum!" Hannah laughed.

"That was the furthest thing from my mind. Can I ask a favour? On the way home, can we stop at the National Memorial Arboretum? I saw the signs on the way down, and I'd like to see it, and pay my respects." Greg was touched at this request. They showered and dressed. Hannah in a pale blue, long dress and high heels. Greg in jeans and t shirt.

"I really must get some new clothes!" he muttered when he saw Hannah.

The journey along the M1 and then the M6 went smoothly. Greg stayed alert but saw nothing to concern him. Harry called and was updated about Hannah's surname and said he'd get straight on it. Then Jenny called.

"Morning both!" she said, chirpily. "Hope your visit to the Metro Trollops went well?" Hannah burst out laughing.

"Better than I could have believed, Jenny" she said, gradually getting used to the Bluetooth system in the car. "We're going home, via the National Memorial Arboretum. Just a visit, to say thank you."

Jenny said. "Such a lovely thought. Greg's never been there. Your powers of persuasion must be amazing." Greg's eyes rolled but he had to agree, Jenny was right.

"And the Detective Inspector?" he asked.

"Oh Greg, I used my charm on him. He's going to visit you tomorrow. Ten o'clock, if that's ok?"

Greg agreed, and they signed off. At the Stoke Junction, Greg left the motorway and headed for Alrewas. Both were quiet. They parked at the NMA and set off around the impressive place of Remembrance. Both were in awe, and the hours slipped effortlessly past. After a cream tea in the restaurant, they headed home, Hannah falling asleep within minutes.

Chapter 21

Attention from the police

Dardan Flaka sat at his desk. There had been no repercussions against him by Salim, mainly because Flaka had promised to replace the arms and ammunition lost in the fire. Albana had smoothed the way as well. Flaka had made the purchase using Bitcoins, something he left to Albana. A ship containing the goods was due to dock in Holyhead in seven days. Flaka would send Granit and Ismet to monitor the unloading of the container, labelled toys. He chuckled, toys indeed! The container would then be taken to Dardans other warehouse outside Manchester and stored there, unopened, until Salim's people arrived. Flaka felt it safer that way. He, Albana and Salim had made the arrangements over dinner at Flaka's house, unaware that every word was being recorded and fed back to GCHQ. From there it went to The General who passed it to Jenny. She formulated a plan which was shared with Greg. Flaka decided to have an early night and kissed his daughter on the cheek.

"Goodnight Daughter" he whispered, "Sleep well."

She waved him away casually. Dardan was not normally a fatherly person but recently he'd been more paternal. It surprised her but not overly. She knew the shipment was the most important deal her father had ever made. To save face and, she believed, his life. These Jihadi scum were dangerous and she needed to be very careful. That is why she had decided to follow the container to Manchester. She didn't trust her father's two favourite thugs.

The next morning, Greg and Hannah arose at seven a.m. and ate a light breakfast. Greg suggested they have a run before the Detective arrived and so they changed into their running gear. The weather was cool but dry and they set off from the gate. Once in the village, they turned left onto the main road. They passed the pub and a forest before following the railway line. Two miles later, they arrived in a small hamlet and Greg took them along a path beside the church. Once past, they set off across fields full of sheep until they reached the road to home. There they turned left and Greg upped the speed until they were both sweating. They raced each other through the open gate and up the lane. This time, neither won the race. They laughed and went into the house. Hannah took first shower with Greg having to wait for his. On the route, Greg had spotted the dark blue Ford Mondeo that passed them twice. While he waited for Hannah to shower, he pondered the fact that he was being watched.

'This could be an interesting meeting.' He thought.

Hannah dressed in her tracksuit and, after showering, so did

Greg. Harry arrived a few minutes later and they sat in the kitchen, coffee in hand, waiting. The trio did not have long to wait. The gate guard radioed through that the police officers had arrived. Greg stayed where he was, Sav at his side. When the car stopped outside, Sav growled.

"Easy pal" Greg said and went to greet the visitors. He opened the door and looked at the officers. Downey was easy to place, tall, stocky, short pepper and salt hair, smart suit. Burrows was more like the poor relative. Tweed jacket, corduroy trousers, old brown shoes. Greg stepped forward and greeted each man in turn, by name. This was designed to put them off balance but he noted that his ruse failed. Downey simply smiled.

"Mr Angel, pleased to meet you, at last."

Greg raised his eyebrow,

"At last?" he said.

Downey ignored the question.

"Nice place you have here. Owned it long?"

Greg noted the Northern Irish accent and bridled.

"Ten years or so. Built in 1872 by a shepherd. Sheep are popular around here. Enlarged over the years by his family. Sold several times, eventually to me."

Downey smiled,

"With close to fifty acres?"

"Close" Greg responded, "Come in."

As they entered the kitchen, Sav growled. Greg failed to say 'friend' and the dog simply looked at the visitors. Gore looked at Harry and Hannah,

"Your solicitor, Greg?" he asked.

"Business partners." Greg said, emphasising the 's'. Downey smiled and introduced them both. Neither rose to shake hands, another ploy by Greg. Gore noted the insult.

"Coffee?" Harry offered. Both declined and Greg invited them into the conservatory, Sav trailing the group closely. Burrows was nervous,

"Is that dog dangerous?" he asked Hannah. She smiled,

"Depends on how you behave" and Greg had a smile to himself.

'Nice,' he thought.

The group sat on the comfortable leather settees and Burrows took a note book from his inside jacket pocket. Gore nodded in approval.

"What exactly does TEAM stand for, Mr Angel?" Downey asked.

"Trusted, Ethical, Asset, Management." Greg said.

Downey continued, after Burrows had made a note in his book.

"Mr Angel, we need to ask you some questions. Is that alright?"

Greg nodded but asked his own question, first,

"Why were you following us on our run?"

This time, Gore was surprised.

"We were recceing the area" he replied.

Greg nodded. "Smart move. Ask away."

Gore spoke first.

"Do you know Dardan Flaka?"

"Never met him" Greg countered.

"With respect, Mr Angel, that's not what I asked. Do you know him?"

"Yes, Detective Inspector, or, rather, I know of him. Through Hannah here. She had a little, er, trouble with him. I was able to help her out."

Gore looked at Hannah.

"Sorry? You are the homeless girl?"

Hannah could only chuckle,

"Yes Inspector. Or rather, I was. Thanks to Greg here, I'm not homeless anymore."

Gore nodded,

"I'm glad to hear it. Mr Angel, did you assault two of

Flaka's employees?"

Greg roared with laughter,

"Employees? Hired thugs. They jumped me and I defended myself. CCTV will prove it. And, of course, Hannah is a prime witness. It'll never get to court. Now then, if that's all you travelled all this way to ask, I'll bid you good day" and he stood.

Gore, however, was not finished,

"And, where were you on Saturday afternoon and evening?"

Greg remained standing,

"Right here, Inspector. I think we had Beef Stifado, didn't we Hannah?"

Hannah nodded,

"Yup, and bloody nice it was too."

Gore smiled and nodded at Burrows.

"You've quite the set up here Mr Angel. Security guards, cctv, etc. Is all that really necessary in your, erm, line of business?"

It was Harry who answered.

"We're in the Security business, Inspector. All those you mentioned, constitute Security."

"I take it you sell security systems, then?" Burrows ventured.

"Yes. And security personnel, advice, technology solutions. There's some valuable stuff here, Sergeant." Harry said.

Gore posed a thoughtful question,

"Are you all ex-military?"

Again, it was Harry who responded,

"Yes, apart from, obviously, Hannah here."

Gore retaliated quickly,

"So, why can't we in the police get any of your records?"

"Restricted, Inspector," Greg said, "Now, if you'll excuse us, we have business to discuss. Thank you for coming." And he moved towards the door. But Gore wasn't finished,

"RUC, Mr Angel?" he asked, looking at the montage, "Know any of those in this picture?"

Greg held his temper, but only just. Hannah rose, and stood beside him as he answered,

"Every fucking one, Inspector, Every. Fucking. One. Harry, show these 'gentlemen' out!" and went into his bedroom, Hannah just behind him. The officers left the house without bidding them farewell. Gore was rattled. When in the car, he turned to Paddy,

"I want everything on that bastard, Paddy, and I mean everything!"

Burrows nodded but remained silent. Not even McReanor

had got under his boss's skin in that way. There would be trouble ahead, he could feel it.

In the bedroom, Hannah held Greg close, saying nothing. Gradually, he calmed down.

"Downey and I will never be drinking buddies" he told her, "I'm sorry for getting rattled. He's a dangerous adversary, more so than Flaka. I'll need to tread carefully."

Hannah kissed him,

"We, Greg, we!"

Greg smiled,

"Yes, The pair of us. I hated the way he looked at you. Like a spider checking out a fly. Let's eat, then we need to plan your future."

As they emerged, Harry was shutting the front door. He studied his friend and boss and was relieved to see calm. Hannah was a good influence on Greg.

Hannah, Harry and Greg sat in the conservatory. Greg had recovered his composure and held Hannah's hand. He told Harry that Hannah had chosen her new surname and Harry showed no surprise when he heard it.

"No problem boss, I'll sort it out. Hannah, do you have a Birth Certificate?"

Hannah nodded,

"Yes, it's the only thing I have. I'll get it." And she left the room. Harry looked at Greg,

"Can you see where this is going mate?" he asked. "I mean, she idolises you. Is that such a good thing?"

Greg smiled,

"Harry, old son, I'll put it simply. I love her and I think she loves me. I've never felt so good in my life. We have what we have. Since the day I first saw her, I've felt a burning need to know her. Now I do. It really is as simple as that."

Hannah refrained from entering the conservatory, having heard what Greg had said. She waited.

It was Harry who spoke next.

"Greg, the fact that you two are in love is not up for argument. We all saw that. And the TEAM are happy for you both. Every man here will fight and, if necessary, die for you both. Just marry her will you!"

Greg chuckled.

"I've been married Harry. That went well, eh? Why would I ruin her life by proposing?"

Just then Hannah returned, a cheerful smile on her face.

"Here we go, Harry" she said, "One Birth Certificate. Sorry it's a bit worn."

Harry accepted the offered piece of paper.

"Not a problem, Hannah Angel!" he said. "A bank account, driving licence, provisional, will be here within a few days. Now then, lovebirds, please excuse me. Nikki says she needs to talk to me. God knows what about, probably about me spending so much time with Greg, here!"

With that, Harry left the couple. Sav sat by Hannah, gazing adoringly into her eyes. She recognised this and said to Greg,

"Greg, Sav is so sweet, can we take him for a walk?"

Hearing the 'walk' word, Sav sat up and trotted to the door. Strolling around his land, Greg was thoughtful. Harry's comments troubled him. He turned to Hannah, saying,

"Hannah, are you happy?"

"What a silly question, Greg" she replied, softly. "I've never been happier."

Greg nodded and stopped walking.

"Good. I'm glad." And he took her in his arms.

They held each other, until Sav brought a tennis ball and dropped it at the feet of Hannah.

"See?" Greg said, "Even Sav loves you."

Hannah and Greg played throw the ball for ages until Greg said,

"Enough! You two young people are tiring me out!"

Hannah laughed,

"Can't have that!" she said, a saucy smile on her face. "Dinner and then, erm, an early night?"

Greg agreed and they headed home.

Chapter 22.

Baptism of fire.

The pair spent the next few days training Hannah on weapons, self-defence and strategy. She was a keen and able learner and they got even closer. Hannah gradually opened up about her time on the streets. Various agencies had tried to 'help' her, but that meant living with drug addicts and prostitutes and she had rebelled. Quite why she had immediately trusted Greg, Hannah didn't know.

Hannah looked at the weapons in the cellar and asked Greg which was his favourite weapon.

Greg didn't hesitate.

"The SLR" he announced, taking the rifle from its resting place.

"Officially called the L1A1 Self-Loading Rifle. It was the weapon of choice for the British Army back in the 70's. Based on the Belgian FN, we Brits endorsed it way back. It weighs about nine pounds, and when the SA80 replaced it, that was a sad day. The SLR fires a 7.62 mm round, compared to the SA80 5.56. The SLR had stopping power, the SA80 was pathetic compared. I fired the G2 at the RSA, Enfield, Royal Small Arms Factory and liked it. Every country used the SLR and most of the British one's were sold off to Africa. Most were semi-automatic, but, a matchstick could alter that. We had twenty rounds in a magazine. In our small range, we can't fire it. However, my sweet, we can go to an ex-military range soon and you can have a go. It's in Hereford, and I've arranged a treat for you."

Hannah nodded. Over the next couple of days, they bonded well. Then Greg announced,

"We're going to Hereford."

Hannah said nothing, just waited. On the Wednesday they set off, full of joy and hope. Arriving in Hereford, Greg turned down a lane that looked as if it hadn't been used in years. Both wore their combat clothes which was just as well. As they drove along, suddenly men burst from every direction, surrounding their Landrover. Greg smiled.

"Saw you way back Corporal!" he called. A tall, well-built man stepped out from behind a bush.

"Bollocks Mr Angel," he called, "Not a fecking chance!"

Greg said,

"One hundred yards in. Sight showing. Two hundred yards in, your fecking moustache!"

The Corporal laughed.

"Sir, it's a pleasure to see you back. Business or pleasure?" Then he saw Hannah. "Oh, forgive me Ma'am!" he said, bowing slightly. "How can we help, Greg?"

"Is the Colonel in? I'd like to borrow the range for a few hours. I've brought my own weapon and ammo."

The Corporal climbed into the back of the car,

"Straight ahead then, Greg. I'm sure the Colonel will be only too happy to oblige."

Greg drove through the gates and followed the Corporal's directions. Once at the Officer's Mess, Greg and Hannah were left waiting in the small reception. Hannah looked around,

"What camp is this?" she asked.

"This is Sterling Lines, home of 22 Special Air Service, Hannah." He replied, sombrely. Just then, the Commanding Officer, Colonel James Stewart, arrived and shook Greg's hand enthusiastically,

"Greg!" he beamed, "How the Devil are you?" Greg answered,

"I'm well, Sir, and you?"

"Oh the usual, nothing ever changes. Now then, who is this young lady?"

Greg did the introductions and Hannah smiled.

"So" said the Colonel, "How can I help you?"

Greg explained that he'd brought his personal SLR and ammunition and wished to use the range for a couple of hours. The Officer considered his request before making his decision,

"I agree, but with one proviso. Whilst I'm aware of your skills, Greg, you will be using MoD property and, as such, need to have an army weapons instructor train Hannah. How does that sound?"

"As long as I'm there too, Sir, I agree."

"Top Man!" the Colonel boomed, "Now then, can you guess who is in camp today, of all days?"

Greg shook his head, "No, Sir, I honestly have no idea!"

The Colonel smiled,

"Sgt Tim Rowlands!"

Greg and Hannah looked at him,

"Tiny Tim?" Greg gasped, "No wonder he slunk off the TEAM HQ! Crafty sod!"

Hannah looked puzzled,

"But I thought none of you were serving any longer?"

Greg chuckled,

"We're allowed to pop back for training purposes. Tim never said a word. What is he doing here Colonel?"

"Training. Not himself, but a new bunch attempting Selection. He's up at the ranges now. Off you pop, oh and Greg, best get yourself and Hannah changed into kit. There will be some at the Range Hut. Have a good time, and lovely to meet you Hannah."

With that he about turned smartly and strode back to his office.

Greg and Hannah left the Mess and drove towards a fenced area, showing a red flag. At the gate, they dismounted and showed their visitors pass that the Corporal had given them. Ahead, Greg saw the butts and, at the firing point, six soldiers in the prone position, Tiny Tim a hulk standing over them. Greg removed his SLR, still in a rifle case, and handed it to Hannah. He then picked up five boxes of ammunition and called out,

"Hello on the Range, Visitors abroad!"

Tim shouted the troops to cease fire and turned around, annoyed that someone had disturbed him. His annoyance soon went when he spotted Hannah and he sprinted over, scooping her up and hugging her.

"My dear Hannah!" he said, "What on earth are you doing here?"

Greg explained and Tim dismissed the bemused recruits.

"Grab a NAAFI break, you lot. Back here in two hours."
From a small shack, Tim handed them a set of coveralls each, in

what is called DPM (Disruptive Pattern Material. The two quickly slipped them on and Tim led them to the firing position. Greg took a back seat here; Hannah was in good hands. For the next two hours, Tim showed Hannah how to strip and reassemble the rifle, patiently explain how every part worked and why. Then he showed her how to load a magazine with 7.62 rounds and where it fitted on the rifle. When he was confident she had that right, he moved on to firing. He stood and took the rifle, brought it up into the aim position and squeezed the trigger. Hannah blanched at the first sound but remained calm as the big man emptied the magazine into a target. Every round hit. He applied the safety catch and turned to Hannah,

"There you go, my dear, nothing to it. Now then, to get used to the weight and the kick back, don't aim. Simply hold the SLR at the waist, safety off, and squeeze the trigger." Greg handed Tim a fully loaded magazine and stepped back. Hannah looked back at him, slightly concerned. Greg winked at her,

"You'll be fine" he said. She turned back to the target and, gripping the rifle for all it's worth, took the safety catch off and pulled the trigger. The rifle barked and rose upwards in her hands but she swiftly lowered it again as round after round flew down range. None hit the target but, as Tim told her, that didn't matter. Getting the feel of the weapon was paramount. Hannah carried out the same procedure with a further four magazines before she felt comfortable. Tim moved on a stage and got her lying in the prone position, flat on her stomach, legs slightly spread behind her. Taking a full mag from Greg, she loaded and squinted along the weapon, trying to line up the rear and foresights. Safety off, she gently squeezed the trigger. Her aim was good but missed the target. Tim took the weapon from her and made a slight adjustment to the front sight.

"Try that" he said, and Hannah resumed her position. Again, she squinted along the weapon and squeezed. The Fig 11 target shook as the round hit it, dead centre of the chest. She fired again and all nineteen rounds scored hits. Putting the safety catch on, Hannah stood, handed the weapon to Tim and jumped at Greg.

"Oh my God!" she exclaimed, "That was amazing. Thank you Tim, thank you so much!"

She went through a further one hundred rounds before Greg called a halt.

"Tim, I can't thank you enough mate." The big man smiled,

"If those wannabes had seen that they'd RTU immediately!" he chuckled, then explained to Hannah that RTU meant Return to Unit. Changing back into their own clothes, Greg and a very excited Hannah climbed back into the Landrover. Greg placed the SLR in the boot, covering it with a blanket. They bade Tim farewell and drove home, not stopping. As Greg explained,

"With an SLR and ammo in the boot, best not to take chances."

On arrival at home, Hannah and Greg let Sav out. He greeted them enthusiastically. Hannah decide she need a shower but Greg stopped her.

"First thing is to clean the SLR. It'll give you practice in stripping and reassembling it." He took her down into the cellar and handed her a cleaning kit. He watched as she expertly took the weapon apart, cleaned and oiled it, then reassembled it again. He nodded,

"Excellent, honestly. Hannah, you are a natural." He placed the weapon back in its gun cabinet and locked it.

"Now then, you shower, I'm cooking!" She kissed him quickly and ran to the shower room. Greg went into the kitchen, fed Sav and set about the cooking. Something stodgy, he decided.

He settled on potato dauphinoise and got going, after pouring himself a celebratory glass of white wine. He could hear Hannah singing in the shower and looked at his faithful canine companion. Sav lay just inside the kitchen door, ears cocked, almost as if he too was listening to the lovely voice. Greg chuckled,

"Yes mate, you're right. That is a great sound to hear." He fussed the dog and gave him a treat from the cupboard. By the time the dinner was in the oven, Hannah emerged from her shower and so Greg took his. After he had finished, he went into the conservatory. Hannah was sitting, legs tucked under her, reading 'The Dandelion Clock', a serene look on her face. Greg took out his phone and quickly took a photo.

Hannah screamed, "NO! I hate having my photo taken."

Greg sat beside her and showed her the photo, taken three years previously and then the one he had just taken.

Pointing at the first picture, he said,

"One week ago. Then today. Hannah, see the real you? You were beautiful then; you just didn't show it. Tonight, the REAL you are sitting here, next to me, the luckiest man alive."

Hannah had tears in her eyes as she spoke,

"I'm the luckiest woman alive, Greg. Honestly I am. Thank you." And she kissed him. They sat in silence for a moment before Greg asked about the book. Hannah was enthusiastic about it.

"I love this writer," she said, "So passionate about her subject, and the characters leap off the page at you."

Greg agreed, he'd read every one of Rebecca Brynn's books. They all held the same passion and attention to detail. It was then that Hannah asked a question that was concerning her.

"Greg, why no television?"

Greg studied her beautiful face,

"I don't watch television. The news is always biased, the BBC is ridiculous and the programmes are mostly repeats. But, if you would like to, we'll go tomorrow and get one?"

Hannah shook her head, "No. I was just curious. I haven't watched a tv programme for years, I doubt we're missing anything. Do you have a TEAM website?"

Greg shook his head, "No, word of mouth is how we get business. That way we don't get junk mail or scammers. We also don't get unwanted attention. Anyone can go online these days and there are some real head cases out there."

She nodded, "ok, just wondered. Thanks for today. That's the most excitement I've had in a long time. The SAS Colonel was nice. How do you know him?"

Greg put on his best Sean Connery voice and said,

"If I told you, I'd have to kill you!"

Hannah roared with laughter,

"Great Jimmy Stewart impression!" and jumped up, still laughing. She ran into the kitchen where Greg finally caught her, took her in his arms and said,

"That was Liam Neeson!"

She roared with laughter again, then became serious and held him tight.

"I'm not dreaming am I Greg?" she asked.

He held her tight and whispered,

"If you are, then so am I"

Just then, the oven pinged, announcing that dinner was ready. They reluctantly released each other and Greg served. Hannah sniffed approvingly,

"Ooh, potato Dauphinoise! I love this."

They ate at the table, a comfortable silence between them.

Tomorrow would be another day.

The next morning, Greg slipped out of bed quietly and went into the kitchen. He wanted to surprise Hannah with a meal that any veteran of Northern Ireland would remember fondly. Called an 'egg banjo', it consisted of a fried egg in a buttered bread bap or bun, liberally coated with the sauce of choice. Named a 'banjo' because, if the egg yolk was runny, it would invariably run down the front of the Flak Jacket, and the method of brushing it off, resembled playing a banjo. Every army unit in Northern Ireland, back then, had a 'choggie' shop. These guys, Indians primarily, worked 24/7 to keep the unit fed and watered. Greg, and many others, held these guys in the highest regards. Coming in from a long, wet patrol, probably having been shot at, or bricked, and finding an egg banjo with a steaming hot cup of coffee, could lift morale beyond words. While the eggs were frying, Greg made a pot of coffee. He prepared the breakfast, placed it onto a tray and went back to the bedroom. Hannah was sitting up.

"I was just about to get up" she said, not meaning a word of it! She had heard the coffee maker and smelled the eggs and had waited patiently. Greg explained about the banjo and, true to form, Hannah dripped egg yolk down the front of her pyjama top. They both laughed as she played 'Duelling Banjo's' and licked her fingers.

Then they both got dressed into their running gear and left the house. Rain had fallen overnight and was threatening to do so again. As Greg told Hannah,

"If it ain't raining, it ain't training!" They ran faster this morning; Hannah was getting very fit now and Greg wanted that to continue. A good diet and plenty of exercise had seen the waif like girl become a woman with a great physique. Gym work had increased that and both were extremely happy. Just as they arrived in the centre of Caernarfon, Greg's phone rang. Hannah burst out laughing! Greg had downloaded 'Stronger' by George Ezra and it was the first time she'd heard it. They stopped by a low wall as Greg responded.

"Jenny! You sound like you're in a wind tunnel!"

He listened for a moment and laughed,

"How long?" Again he listened, before hanging up.

"Jenny is flying in to see us." He told Hannah.

"Flying in? Should we meet her at the airport?" Greg chuckled,

"No, my sweet. She's coming by helicopter. I need to put the 'H' out in the field," and set off running. Hannah shook her head then took off after him. This she simply did NOT want to miss!

They set a fast pace on the way home and they became aware of a helicopter hovering some two hundred metres to the east. The chopper was a Gazelle, otherwise known as the 'whistling chicken leg'. Normally used as an observation and reconnaissance helicopter, it had proved invaluable in Northern Ireland in the 70's. Agile, it had excellent visibility from the cockpit. Smiling at each other, they knew Jenny would be watching and the pace was ramped up dramatically. They sped along the road to the house and through the gate, pounding up the track, arriving at the front door together. Greg puffed,

"Bloody hell, woman! That was some run for my money." He heard the chopper coming and trotted towards the centre of the field, only to see the gate guard had pegged out the white 'H' for Jenny to land. He raised his hand in the gate direction in acknowledgement. He and Hannah waited as the helicopter flared and lowered towards the ground, once landed, the blades wound down slowly. Hannah rather expected Jenny to be the pilot and was mildly disappointed to see she was just a passenger. When the blades sat still, Jenny left the craft and joined them, wearing full DPM kit, a briefcase held across her chest. No headwear which left her shiny blonde hair to fall to her waist. As she approached the pair, she called out,

"Congratulations, Hannah! There's not many can match Greg in a sprint after a five-mile run. You'll have to watch her Greg; you'll be playing catch up soon!"

Hannah blushed with pride and Greg smiled.

"That day will come sooner than I expect!" he said, "I'll have to be on my guard."

They walked towards the door and Sav, sitting outside, ignored Jenny, but ran to Hannah for a fuss. Jenny looked on,

"That young lady is quite remarkable, Greg. The General has told me of your visit to Hereford. I have a feeling Hannah is going to be a vital TEAM member, and soon!"

Once inside, Hannah made coffee then the three sat at the table. Jenny briefed them.

"Flaka has a new consignment of arms and ammunition arriving on a container vessel into Holyhead Container Port on Sunday. When are your guys back?" she asked Greg.

"All here by midday Saturday," Greg assured her, "Raring to go. I've a couple of contracts I'm going to sub out for next week. Straight forward bodyguard work."

Jenny nodded, and continued,

"Good. Now then, as I said, the container arrives here approx. 06.00 on Sunday but won't be ready to be unloaded until roughly twelve hours later. Flaka is sending Granit and Ismet to follow it. Albana, being the untrusting sort, will be following them!" The three laughed.

"Now here's the rub. Being as we knew about this, there's been a switch of containers. Flaka's will hold nothing but toys from China. Same colour container, same tare weight etc, and same security seal, so nothing will look out of place. We will let them go, then, when it's quieter, two of our men will drive up, load the real container, and take it off. That, my dear Greg, is where you come in. I know you still hold your HGV Licence but I would rather Tim and Legs took the truck, with the rest of your team following."

Hannah looked on, impressed with the amount of planning involved here,

"Where too?" she asked. Jenny looked at her,

"Well, Hannah, we are planning a small demonstration for Mr Flaka. When the fake container arrives at the Manchester warehouse, Special Branch, along with Counter Terrorism, will surround and seize it, along with Granit and his brother. Albana will be ignored, just so she can tell her father. They will wait for two hours, then they, along with your team, will raid Flaka's home. You'll be sorted with your task by then, Greg. You will have loaded the container containing the arms etc, onto another ship. During the voyage, there will be an accident and the container will topple into the sea, never to be seen again. I need your team to make sure it gets loaded, can't trust anyone else."

Greg nodded. "Sounds good to me. On raiding Flaka's house, are we going in armed?"

"Wearing, but not waving around. Flaka has a good cctv system set up. He'll more than likely be watching from wherever he's hiding and we want him to see that you, and Hannah, are with us. Then, after you've appeared to be in charge, we notice the cctv and disable it. I'm hoping it will send him a strong message to leave you both alone."

Over the next hour, the three discussed everything from uniform to vehicles to tactics for the Sunday. Hannah found herself getting very excited. She spoke her thoughts,

"Greg, Jenny, am I too soon to hope that, after Sunday, Greg and I can get on with our lives? I mean, will this nightmare finally be over?" Her voice caught as she spoke and Greg held her hand. But it was Jenny who spoke,

"Hannah, if that bastard doesn't leave you alone after this, I'll kill him myself!"

Jenny took her leave and Greg and Hannah showered and changed. They walked casually down to the local pub and ordered lunch. Greg would continue Hannah's weapons training later but, for now, some quality time was called for.

Over the next couple of days, Greg and Hannah ran, exercised and sparred together, Sav constantly at their sides, even on the run. He was a faithful companion and behaved impeccably. In the gym, Greg put on the sparring mitts and Hannah the boxing gloves. She was lithe, fit and fast, even he had to admit. On one occasion, she caught him out with a low sliding kick to his legs and he went down. Immediately she apologised but Greg waved her away with a laugh.

"Excellent!" he said, "caught me right out there. I'm going to have to watch you!"

The pair grew ever closer and their love making was passionate and caring. They forgot the upcoming mission and immersed themselves into their relationship. All too soon, though, Saturday arrived. They rose early, had a coffee and set off on their run. Sav stayed behind, Greg wanted him there when the TEAM arrived. This time they took a different route. Once on the main road, they turned right, through the village and then right at the crossroads. The hill rose steeply ahead of them and Greg forced the pace, Hannah matching him step for step. At the next junction, Greg continued on, up an even steeper hill, his legs pounding a fast pace. He could feel the muscles in his legs burning but continued. Hannah felt the same but made no complaint. After a mile, they reached a magnificent view point and Greg called a halt. He sat on a large rock, panting.

"See the view Hannah?" he asked. "The Summit of Snowdon is that way" he continued, pointing east, "the Menai Straights the other way. I've not been here for some time. I forgot how beautiful it is."

Hannah nodded, breathing deeply.

"Yes, it's fantastic," she said and sat next to him, "I'll almost be sorry to not have you all to myself, even if just for a short time."

He hugged her, "We have the rest of our lives together, Hannah" he whispered into her ear, "and I intend to make the most of that time."

They slowly walked back down the hill, past a forest which towered above them, no other sound. They also walked the remaining mile home, content to bask in each other's presence. Once there, they showered and changed into their DPM clothes, then Hannah cooked scrambled egg. Greg fed Sav and they were happy.

Harry was the first to arrive, just before eleven o'clock. He helped himself to coffee and Greg updated him on the week and the plan for Sunday.

"I'm coming on this one" Harry said, "you can leave Pilgrem behind this time." Greg agreed. Sepp and Jack arrived next with Legs not far behind. When Tim arrived, he scooped Hannah up and said,

"Morning my little sharp shooter!" much to Hannah's embarrassment. At last, Pilgrem strolled casually through the door and the TEAM was complete. Greg gave a mission update, allocated roles and Hannah suggested they adjourn to the pub, where Greg would buy lunch. Harry agreed it was a superb idea and they got ready. Hannah had an ulterior motive for going to the pub, she had a favour to ask of Tracey. The guys took their gear to the barn and returned a few minutes later. The atmosphere was one of joy as the group strolled casually along the lane, turning down a narrow footpath which was a shortcut to the pub. It was single file all the way and Hannah went in front of Greg, seemingly keen to arrive first. At the end of the path, they turned left onto the road and went into the pub. Tracey greeted them all with enthusiasm, especially Hannah. Once the group were seated, Hannah went to the bar and was in deep conversation with the host. Plenty of nodding and giggles emanated from that area and Greg was curious. When Hannah took her seat, next to him, he asked casually,

"What was that about?" Hannah shook her head,

"Oh no, a surprise!" Tim and the others chuckled loudly,

"Probably champagne boss!" Tim said and Hannah shook her head again.

"No guessing, none of you will have a clue. Except, Greg, Tracey is coming by this afternoon, is that ok?"

Greg assured her that Tracey was welcome any time and they set to ordering their meals.

Harry had been busy during the week and Hannah's bank account details had arrived. She insisted on paying for the lunch happy that the money removed from the drugs mules had been paid into her account. She loved her new found freedom, and thanked Greg for it. He shrugged it off,

"Nothing less than you deserve, Hannah" he said, smiling. They finished their meal and walked back home. Hannah informed Greg that Tracey would arrive in the next half hour and she required the 'boys' as she called them, to make themselves scarce for at least an hour! The 'boys' laughed and Legs remarked,

"Ok little sister, we'll go to the gym, is that ok Greg?" Greg readily agreed.

Right on time, Tracey arrived carrying a large holdall, shielding it from the men.

"Go on you lot, get out of here, this is girls only for the next hour! Scram!"

They quickly made an exit, wondering what the hell was going on. Once in the gym, they each hit a machine and did circuits for well over an hour. Greg dried himself with a large towel and walked back to the house. He knocked and called,

"Safe to come in, ladies?" Tracey replied, "It's safe!"

Greg walked in and through to the conservatory. There, sat demurely on the settee, was a new look, blonde streaked, Hannah. She wore a dark red dress, just finishing above her knees, and black high heel shoes. Greg's mouth dropped. His heart pounded and he stood, too stunned to move or even speak. Tracey took his arm,

"Meet your new Hannah" she said, guiding him forward.

He sat next to Hannah, still unable to talk. Hannah grew worried,

"Don't you like it?" she asked, almost timidly.

He found his voice and croaked,

"Hannah, you get more beautiful every time I see you. I, I, I love it." He stammered.

She hugged him, relieved but also pleased that she could have that effect on the man she had grown to love, albeit in such a short time. Tracey left them to it. Hannah was fast becoming a great friend and Tracey hoped that she and Greg would 'get together'. When the others arrived, they were almost as impressed as Greg had been. Hannah went to change having decided that, that evening, she and Greg were to have a romantic meal together, but not at home.

Hannah had asked Tracey where she could take Greg for a romantic meal, mainly to thank him for everything. Tracey suggested a Greek restaurant in town and had promised to make a reservation when she got back to the pub. This she did and sent a text to Hannah telling her the table for two was booked for eight o'clock at Ouzo and Olive. Hannah thanked her and told Greg. She also asked Tim if he would be their driver, he readily agreed. Greg went to shower and then changed in his bedroom. He took time to choose, wanting to make Hannah proud. Eventually, he chose a dark blue suit, white shirt and his Corps tie. For a finishing touch, he added the Royal Ulster Constabulary tie pin. He'd had it years, but never worn it. Tonight seemed the perfect time. Tim escorted them to the Landrover and opened the back doors. He drove sedately into Caernarfon and slid to a gentle halt outside the restaurant, jumping out and opening the door for Hannah. While they ate and drank, Tim sat in the car in the narrow street, pistol under his thick thigh. Just in case. Hannah and Greg emerged at eleven o'clock and Tim drove them home, via Dinas Dinlle, where the pair strolled, hand in hand, along the beach for a while. Their conversation had been about mundane things and nothing about the past or the future. For this evening, they were an island, two people, deeply in love, not a care in the world, and Tim was going to make sure they had a good time. As they strolled along, hand in hand, the sea lapped the shore gently, just a few feet away. The moon shone on the placid ocean. Hannah turned to Greg,

"Have you any family?" she asked.

Greg paused, his eyes clouding over.

"My parents are both dead. I have a brother, ten years my senior. We don't talk."

"Oh, I'm sorry. Can I ask why you don't see each other?" Hannah wondered.

"If I met him, I'd probably kill him!" Greg replied, no sadness in his voice. "You deserve an explanation. His actions towards me when I was a child would, today, be called bullying and abuse at the very least. Back then it was just 'discipline'. He was an evil bastard and I couldn't wait to leave home. If he was ever on leave at the same time as I was, it was a difficult time."

"He was in the army too?" Hannah asked.

"Nah, not a chance! He joined the RAF Police, what we squaddies call a Snowdrop. He lives in Newark, that's a perfect anagram for him. He certainly won't get an invite to our..." and there he stopped talking, looking deep into Hannah's eyes,

"But now isn't the time for that question." And he kissed her lightly. She smiled, knowing what he wanted to say but hadn't found the right time or place. Her heart beat louder and faster as they walked back to where Tim stood, waiting patiently.

When they returned home, both thanked Tim who seemed embarrassed. He retired to the Bunk House and Greg and Hannah fell, exhausted, into bed.

Chapter 23.

Flaka can't 'contain' himself.

Rain hammered the triple glazed windows of Greg's house. The sky was brooding and dark, clouds scudding across the sky. Sav did his ablutions quickly, while Greg and Hannah sheltered under the porch. Neither spoke a word. Both were physically drained, mostly from their love making the previous night. But they were also reaching their emotional peak. Hopefully, today, Flaka would be removed from their lives. Greg had given the future serious consideration and had come up with a plan, but not one he could, or would, discuss with anyone until later. When Sav trotted in, the couple walked into the kitchen. Soon, the TEAM arrived and were eating the full English Hannah had prepared. It was Sepp, usually the quite one who remarked,

"Hannah, mein Liebchen, if Greg fails to propose soon, then I will!" The rest agreed with Tiny Tim saying,

"Get in the queue my boy, cos I is first after Greg!"

Hannah blushed and said,

"Wow, so many to choose from!" she smiled at Greg, "But there's only one for me. Sorry to disappoint you others!" Now Greg blushed. Tim had known Greg for over fifteen years and his heart went out to him. He'd been with his boss during Northern Ireland and when Miriam had been killed. They had a special bond.

The group discussed the upcoming mission, thrashing out everything that could or would, go wrong. Even Hannah made a contribution, which pleased the TEAM. Everyone laughed when Greg used some of Conner's toy cars and trucks to demonstrate the plan. Then they got ready, each dressing for their part. Once all complete, they set off, in a variety of vehicles. The two fake Open Reach vans were now plain white and Tim and Legs took one. Pilgrem remained behind, manning the radios. Greg and Hannah went in the Landrover, Sepp and Jack in a white van. Hannah and Greg wore DPM's under raincoats. The convoy set off in good spirits.

They reached a motorway services on the A55 at Penmaenmawr an hour later. Jenny had arranged for two plain white Scania tractor units to be parked there. Tim and Legs jumped into one and set off for Holyhead Container Port to collect the real container. They rolled into the loading area an hour later and waited in the queue. Legs called Greg, chuckling,

"Guess who we're parked immediately behind?" he asked. Greg guessed correctly that it was Granit and Ismet and laughed out loud.

"Keep a low-profile Legs, remember, they might not have met you but they can smell trouble a mile off."

Thirty minutes later, they received word that the Albanians had left, with the bogus consignment. Another thirty minutes and Legs and Tim were on their way back. Greg, Hannah and Jack had stayed in the Landrover until now. Greg climbed out and chatted to Harry and Sepp.

"As soon as Legs gets back, swap units and take the container back." He gave Harry the return paperwork and shook his hand.

"God speed, old son" he said.

At that point, Jenny called. The Armed Response Unit was behind the Albanians. They had also noticed a black motorbike, keeping pace. It looked as if Flaka didn't trust his two henchmen and had sent Albana to keep tabs. The ARV dropped back and swapped with several other unmarked units so as to avoid suspicion. Greg felt elated. So far, so good. But a plan is only a success until contact with the enemy. Then it can all go to rat shit! Just over an hour later, Tim and Legs rolled in, parked next to Harry and Sepp and climbed out. They dropped the legs on the trailer, then moved aside while Harry, expertly, reversed onto the trailer. Once the fifth wheel clunked, Sepp raised the legs and they rolled out. Tim and legs got into one of the white vans and sat patiently. Their role was, effectively, over, but they wanted to be in at the arrest. Tim called Greg over and asked the question. Greg thought about it and agreed, as long as they kept well back. Tim punched the air in delight. Legs merely chuckled,

"Tim, you never change mate, and for that, I'm glad!" he said.

It took a further two hours for Harry and Sepp to return. They had been stopped by VOSA and had their vehicle checked. They had almost missed their slot but made it with minutes to spare, courtesy of Sepp sweet talking the VOSA lady Inspector. They parked their unit next to the other one, left the keys under the fifth wheel and boarded the second white van. Greg informed them that they could be in at the arrest of Flaka and could even line the street and wave him off, in handcuffs. This brought about an almighty cheer from everyone and Hannah hugged Greg.

"What a fantastic idea" she said. They climbed into the Landrover with Jack driving and set off; the two white vans very close behind. Whilst jubilant, the atmosphere was one of caution, this being the most dangerous part. They kept their speed down, not wanting to overtake their enemies who would be travelling at no more than sixty and may well have stopped for a break. Greg called Jenny for an update. All was on schedule though. The container had reached the warehouse and Granit and Ismet had left the building. Albana had disappeared and Jenny was worried. She brought the arrest time forward an hour, which was ok for Greg and his TEAM. They stepped up the speed and raced towards Wilmslow. As they neared, Jack pulled to the side of the road and Greg and Hannah removed their coats, revealing their DPM uniform. Jack handed them both a belt with a holster. In the holsters were Browning 9mm Hi Power pistols. The pair removed the magazines and cleared the breech. Once sure the weapons were clear, they loaded them and cocked, effectively putting a round into the breech. Safety catches on, they were ready to roll. Greg called Jenny and she said they were five minutes from Flaka's house and to meet them there. The Armed Response would gain entry and then Jenny, Greg and Hannah would storm in and effect the arrest. Exactly four minutes later, two ARV's, one Landrover, two white vans and a BMW i8 swarmed into the huge driveway of Flaka's impressive mansion. Six armed cops raced to the front door, battering ram ready but that was not needed. The door was opened by a flunky who was quickly subdued and handcuffed. The officers raced in, checking every room, shouting 'Clear' at each. Jenny, Greg and Hannah walked in, disappointment on their faces.

"The bastard's not here!" Jenny stormed. "Fuck!"

Greg looked around and noticed, in the corner of the hallway, a camera, red light blinking on top. He realised that Flaka was watching them from somewhere and walked over to it. Greg unfastened his holster and removed his pistol. Hannah followed his actions. Then they both pointed their weapons at the camera. Their faces were uncovered and showed their anger. Greg spoke into the camera,

"Flaka. You know Hannah and now you know me. I'm coming for you."

With that, they left the house and drove away, nobody speaking.

Chapter 24.

A strategic withdrawal.

Dardan Flaka sat in the office above his club, watching the cctv screen. He realised he had made a serious error of judgement. Angel was not just an adversary, he was one to be wary of, and respected. Hannah on the other hand, puzzled him. How the hell had that homeless waif changed so much in such a short time? Unless she was undercover? No, he discounted that. Angel must have given her some training. That alone worried him. The professional way they had pointed their pistols at the camera showed Flaka he was outgunned. He also realised that the arms and ammunition he had transported had been compromised. He had only one option. A strategic withdrawal. His funds were safe in off shore accounts that even the FBI couldn't touch if they tried. No, that was the least of his problems. Escaping the country might prove difficult, until he thought of his yacht. Moored in Mayflower marina, Plymouth, it would take time to get there but that was not his problem. The 400 berth fully serviced Marina was located overlooking Mt Edgecumbe Country Park and Flaka had rarely been there. He had a full staff of ten on permanent standby, time for them to earn their money. His yacht was a Leopard 53 Powercat. With four spacious cabins, it had seemed perfect for Flaka. There was plenty of room but he'd only cruised around for a few days in it. The Powercat was 16 metres in length by 7 metres beam. Its draft was less than one metre which made it ideal for all seas and almost all weathers. He immediately called his Captain and gave him orders. Albana entered the room and stood, hands on hips.

"So, we run eh?" she snapped.

"We withdraw, my daughter, not run. We will be back, this I promise. Then that Angel will be a dead angel!"

"Where we go, eh?" Albana retorted, "To hide from one fucking MAN!"

Dardan stood and approached her. He then did something he had never done before. He slapped her, hard, across the cheek. She stood rock still, waiting for the next strike, but it didn't arrive. Instead, he hugged his daughter.

"We take a step back, to take two steps forward. Our interests in Greece have been neglected. Time to reflect, to plan and to have our revenge. In six months, we return, but only when you have delivered a crushing blow to this Crusader."

The promise pacified her, for the moment.

Chapter 25.

Planning for the future.

For the TEAM, the journey home was taken in complete silence. Two hours and not one word spoken. The atmosphere in each vehicle was palpable. Greg brooded silently, his mind in a turmoil. How did Flaka know? Pure luck? Greg doubted that, there must have been a leak. Then his mind switched to the future. Every one of the guys were booked on specific jobs in just two days' time. Greg had hoped to have had this situation wrapped up by then. Now, they were in limbo. He wondered where Flaka was. What he was doing. How he was feeling. As they approached home, he made a decision. The vehicles stopped outside the house and Greg stormed inside, Hannah following. The guys had seen Greg in this mood before and knew to leave well alone, so they were surprised when their boss called them inside. He ordered them into the conservatory and went into the kitchen. He returned with cans of beers and a bottle of white wine, glasses and beer jugs. Hannah sat on one settee, Sav curled up beside her. Greg normally didn't allow him on the furniture but decided to let it go this time. He handed out the beers to the guys, with jugs, and poured two glasses of wine for himself and Hannah, then sat down, away from Hannah. She looked at Tim, a worried expression on her pretty face. Tim shrugged, completely perplexed. He had expected an explosion of anger and the lack of it worried him. Greg took a drink of his wine, then topped his glass up. Tim's eyebrows raised. Still no one spoke. Then Greg did.

"Guys, and Hannah, today was both a success and a failure. We had the success, Jenny the failure. I raise my glass in a toast to you all. But also to that Albanian bastard, for outwitting me. It won't happen again. Wherever he is, I'll find him. But not today. I have a question to ask one of you."

Each looked at the other, not having a clue what was coming next. Greg took a deep breath.

"Hannah." He said, pausing. She looked petrified and said nothing. Greg continued, eventually,

"Hannah. In a short time, you have come to mean more to me than anyone else ever has." He paused again, taking a deep breath. Tim glanced at the girl and saw her eyes water. He smiled encouragingly, but she didn't notice.

"Hannah" Greg continued, a pause between every word. "Hannah, would you do me the honour of becoming my wife?"

The room was silent for what seemed like several minutes. Greg thought he'd played this wrong and took another long drink, before reaching over and topping his glass up, yet again.

Every face in the room looked at Hannah, seemingly even Sav. She sat stock still, tears running down her cheeks, breathing deeply, unable to respond. Finally, she regained her composure and replied,

"Yes!"

The room erupted with cheers, whoops and shouts of congratulations! Hannah ran to Greg, took his glass of wine from him, sat on his lap and shouted, at the top of her voice,

"YES!"

It was then that Greg broke down, holding her tight and crying his heart out. He sobbed on her shoulder, his emotions running riot. He was so happy, yet so sad. He thought of Miriam and his sobs became racking, until, embarrassed, he wiped his eyes and said,

"Sorry guys, got a little emotional there. Harry, be a lad and get more beers in. Oh, and another bottle of wine, I seem to have drunk most of this one!"

The group sat and raised their glasses to the happy couple. Hannah's cheeks were rosy with excitement, Greg's face looked drawn, as if he'd just experienced some traumatic event. It was Harry who had the idea.

"Folks, firstly I wish to congratulate the extremely happy couple." There were more cheers. Harry called for silence,

"Now listen, today needs to be forgotten, apart from the

proposal, that is!" This brought laughter and he went on,

"I am now ordering each and every one of you to the pub!" More cheers.

Greg nodded,

"I suggest Hannah and I get changed first, Harry, can't turn up in DPM's and carrying pistols! Might scare the natives!" With that, he scooped Hannah up into his arms and ran to the bedroom, amid catcalls and cheers. Once inside, they embraced and kissed fervently before breaking off. Still smiling broadly, they quickly changed into jeans and t shirts and returned to the conservatory.

"We'll have to walk. I don't want any of us getting done for drink driving." Tim held them both close and whispered,

"Congratulations boss. And Hannah, I'm so proud of you." Hannah kissed him on the cheek and Greg shook his hand.

The group set off out of the gate in high spirits. Hannah and Greg holding hands, the others chatting animatedly to each other. The entered the pub and Legs called for silence, before announcing the good news! Tracey ran around the bar and clasped them both. Even she had tears in her eyes and ordered that champagne be put on ice, on the house. After a few minutes, Greg and Hannah went outside and smoked a cigarette. Greg asked her, in a worried tone,

"Is it too soon, Hannah?"

She took her time answering.

"No, it took you bloody long enough!" and the pair roared with laughter. Their smoke break completed, they returned to the bar at the rear of the building. Tracey smiled and nodded to Phil, the barman. Instantly, 'Shotgun' by George Ezra filled the room and was soon drowned out by singing voices. Champagne flowed and spirits were high. This, Greg realised, was what the TEAM so desperately needed and tensions eased. He smiled contentedly. Today could have been the worst of his life, but it had become the greatest. Just then his mobile rang. He stepped outside, Hannah following a few seconds later, just in time to hear him ask,

"Who talked!"

Jenny answered abruptly, "A Detective Constable. He charmed one of the Control Room girls who told him about the container. He must have called Flaka straight away. He's in custody and singing like a canary."

Greg sighed, "And Flaka?" he asked, holding his breath.

"Gone. Possibly by boat, certainly not by air. We'll find him, eventually. For now Greg, try to relax. The threat has been removed. Have some fun, although it sounded like you've already started."

Greg handed the phone to Hannah,

"Tell her sweetheart." And walked off, towards the far end

of the car park. He stood looking at the twin mountains only a mile away. He leaned on the wooden rail and lit another cigarette. Hearing footsteps on the gravel, he turned. Hannah walked towards him, unsure whether to smile or not. He took her in his arms.

"Looks like he's fled the country, Hannah" he said, "We can relax a little. Hannah, from now on, your life is going to be one of joy, happiness and pleasure. What did Jenny say?"

"She's pleased for us and, obviously, wants an invite!" she replied, finally able to smile. "I love you Greg" she said quietly, I really do!"

"I love you too Hannah. I mean that with all my heart." And they kissed passionately, the rest of the world forgotten.

The rest of the evening went swimmingly. Plenty of alcohol was consumed and glasses raised to the, by now, embarrassed couple. By the time eleven o'clock arrived, the group were more than slightly intoxicated. All except for Tim, who seemed to have not had any alcohol. But Tim was made of sterner stuff and had vowed not to get drunk, but rather to keep an eye on proceedings. Just in case.

Harry called for a taxi to take him home, the rest retired to the bunkhouse in good spirits. Hannah and Greg collapsed, fully clothed on the bed and immediately descended into a deep and dreamless sleep.

HANNAH

The noise of the mobile ringing awoke Greg just after six next morning. Given the amount of alcohol he had consumed the previous evening, he felt remarkably fresh. Hannah didn't stir beside him and he wondered how they had slept in such uncomfortable positions. Hannah was half on the bottom of the bed and half on the floor, and Greg himself was the same, but reversed. He got to his feet and grabbed his phone.

"Shhh!" he said when he answered, "You'll wake Hannah up!"

He heard a chuckle from the caller,

"Greg my boy! How are you? Slight hangover?" chuckled the General, "Bit of a party last night eh?"

Greg groaned to himself. The last thing he needed right now was an effervescent Officer bawling down the phone at him. He went into the kitchen and switched the coffee machine on.

"Good morning to you too, Sir" he answered, dreading what was coming next.

"I hear congratulations are in order?" was the reply, still chuckling.

"Thank you, yes, she's going to make an honest man of me." Greg threw back.

"Good. Good. Now then, business, and yes I'm aware what day it is. How are your men deployed for the next few weeks, eh?"

PAUL REES

Greg thought hard, "As of Tuesday, all but Harry are on contracts, for the next two weeks. Gives me some time to get my admin in order."

"Excellent, excellent. Now then, we've had word that our friend Flaka has buggered off on his boat, most likely to Europe. It seems Salim is not happy at losing a second consignment of arms and ammunition. Put something of a contract out on Flaka. Your name hasn't shown up, so we're happy with that. Mind, his daughter, Albana may put the spanner in the works on that score. We'll keep GCHQ on the chatter and advise accordingly. One thing, it seems one of the ARV bods recognised you and informed our Detective Inspector Downey. He may get curious, but don't worry, he's a hundred miles away. Right, must dash, the Good Lady is summoning me. Congratulations again to both you and Hannah. Ahem, I trust we'll be invited?"

Greg laughed, "I just knew that was the real reason you called you old rascal! You'll both be top of our list, thanks for calling General." And Greg ended the call. He heard a groan from behind him and turned around. Hannah stood in the doorway, one hand to her head, the other on the door, and she was swaying.

"What hit me?" she mumbled. Greg laughed,

"Ha! You kids! Can't take the pace!" he giggled.

"Fuck off!" was her slightly less than polite response, as she moved towards him, unsteadily. He caught her in his arms and held her close.

"That's no way to talk to your future husband, young lady" he said, kissing her gently.

"Oh my God! You meant it!" she cried, "Really? I didn't dream it?"

"As real as your hangover sweetheart, now sit, I'll bring you a coffee, after I've let poor Sav out."

Five minutes later, they sat in the conservatory, the sun muted through the windows. Hannah sat, head back, trying to recover. Greg went to the computer and onto the internet. He had an idea about the wedding and wanted to see if it was possible. He checked various sites and hit on one. 'There!' He read the words carefully and thumbed a number into his phone. He'd make the call later today. Out of the corner of his eye he saw Harry arriving at the gate. He decided to keep the perimeter guard on for another week. Best to be safe than sorry. Harry arrived and helped himself to coffee and joined them. He looked even worse than Hannah. Greg greeted him warmly.

"Hangover, mate?" he asked, smiling broadly.

"Fuck off!" Harry responded, also smiling, "I should have got a taxi here, I'm sure I'm over the limit."

Hannah chuckled, "You oldies, can't take the pace!"

Harry threw a soft cushion roughly in her direction laughing.

"What's the plan, today then Greg?"

"Wedding plans, mate" Greg replied, looking cautiously at Hannah. "Erm, I'll need some help from you, mate, and Hannah can ask Tracey for help and advice. If that's ok, Hannah?"

She nodded but winced at the effort.

"Yes, Dear!" she said. Although her heart wasn't in it. The physical hangover and the emotions of being proposed to, tried to overwhelm her, but she fought it bravely.

Harry had something else on his mind,

"Flaka?" he asked, and Greg updated them both. "Harry, can you find out where he might be? Downey has gotten wind of our involvement in the failed arrest; he may get curious."

Harry surprised Greg with the answer immediately.

"Greece" he said, "he's got a large villa in Halkidiki, a place called Polichrono. Set apart from the town, on three levels. Fenced off and guarded. The locals hate him and are not happy that he's on his way back. To be honest, mate, I think as long as he stays there, we should put him on the back burner."

Greg reluctantly agreed.

"OK, we'll concentrate on business. Can you get the guys up to speed with their assignments? I'll hit the admin button and show Hannah how the company works." He noted her look, "But that's tomorrow. Today? I'm doing a full English for breakfast. You staying Harry?" Even though he knew the answer. They ate, despite Hannah's protests, and felt better afterwards. The rest of the team gradually arrived and Greg cooked them the same. It was gratefully received. He looked around and muttered,

"What a motley crew!" By the mid-afternoon, all were feeling better and held a meeting. The SAS would call them 'Chinese Parliaments' but, as none present had been in that select group, it remained a meeting. By early evening, the members of the TEAM, minus Greg, Hannah and Harry, were making their goodbyes. It was emotional and Hannah cried. They waved them off and went into the lounge. Greg took Hannah's hand and went to the montage which contained Miriam's picture.

"You were right, Hannah. You are not her. But you are every bit her equal with one exception. You have my love. Miriam only had my friendship."

He touched the photo once and turned away. By helping Hannah, Greg felt he'd made things right with Miriam. Hannah touched the picture also and whispered,

"Thank you Miriam. I'll look after him, I promise."

Chapter 26.

The lull before the Storm.

The next two weeks passed quickly. Greg had no worries about his colleagues. There was no need to chase them for updates. If anything happened, they would take care of things and tell him afterwards. He sought out a local driving instructor and did a deal with him. Greg would pay Aled £500 for a full week's tuition for Hannah and, if she passed her test at the end of that week, Aled would receive a £100 bonus. The instructor took Hannah out on the Monday and reported that she was a natural. Greg was pleased. While she was taking her lessons, Greg and Harry dived into the admin of the company, paying bills, producing invoices and generally tidying up. Every morning, Hannah and Greg went for a run, and in the evenings, they hit the mini gym. Hannah was taking shape nicely. Greg also sorted out the date of the wedding. He had hoped that they could marry during the summer of the following year but his ideal venue was fully booked. However, the Reverend Katy Jones, the Dean of Bangor, told him that she had a space in mid-December. Hannah had said she'd love a church wedding and so Greg booked that date. It would be a week before his birthday and Hannah was thrilled.

"You'll remember our anniversary then!" she joked.

The Cathedral is dedicated to its founder, Saint Deniol and had been a place of Christian worship since the 6th century. Originally a Monastery, it was sacked in 634 and again in 1073. Nothing of the original building survives. Greg had visited the Cathedral many times over the ten years he'd lived in the area, fascinated by the architecture. He considered it the perfect place to commence married life. Hannah looked at it on the internet and agreed. Greg then called Conner and told him the good news. The lad was happy but made one point,

"Don't ask me to be Best Man, Dad. That would involve making a speech and I'm no good at that. Anyway, I'm too far away to help with the organising. Get one of the guys to do it. I'd suggest Tim. I like him, he's fecking awesome!"

Greg reluctantly agreed but waited to ask Tim in person. He asked Harry to sort out the logistics, music and such, and went off to look for a suitable wedding car for Hannah. He also looked for a honeymoon destination but came up blank. After talking it through with his wife to be, they decided to honeymoon the following summer.

All thoughts of Flaka were put to the back of their minds. Their relationship grew even stronger, and they learned to almost know what the other was thinking. This was apparent during sparring sessions, where Hannah was almost Greg's equal in self- defence.

On the Saturday, they drove into Chester and bought the engagement ring. As they stood in the jewellers, both nervous, Greg looked around. Eventually, they chose a swirl Halo ring. It consisted of a centre stone, an Emerald, surrounded by a cluster of diamonds. The ring was 18 carat gold and looked perfect on Hannah's finger. Her beam of joy was a picture to behold and the young lady who served them almost had tears in her eyes as she watched. There was a beautiful elegance to the ring which only served to make Hannah look even more beautiful.

The journey home was in the MG, roof down, singing to romantic songs on the cd player.

While Greg and Hannah were choosing the ring, Jenny sat in a Regency armchair in the lounge of the Generals house. She had accepted the invitation to stay over and was nursing a large whiskey. Dickie looked across at her as he spoke,

"Well, Jenny, what are your thoughts, eh?"

The woman thought carefully before answering,

"Well, Dickie, I never thought things would get this far. I suggest we let things run their course?"

Dickie agreed and the two went through to the spacious dining room for their evening meal, cooked and served perfectly by Sue.

Chapter 27.

The Wedding

Time whizzed past and Hannah and Greg were busy. Hannah went to London with Tracey and chose her wedding dress. Greg insisted that Tim, who was on a few days off, go with them. It was the perfect arrangement. The girls would be safe and Tim and Tracey could spend some time together. Over the weeks, Greg took Hannah on the Welsh Highland Steam Railway, which enthralled her. Then they took the Snowdon Mountain Railway to the summit, before walking back down. For once, the view from the top was clear and both stood, enamoured by nature. Greg whispered,

"Sweetheart, when I die, cremate me and scatter my ashes here, please?"

Hannah looked into his eyes,

"Don't talk like that. Please? But, ok, when the time comes, yes. But do the same for me?"

They embraced, both lost in thought.

They visited other places of interest at the weekends. Greg

had been pleased when Hannah had passed her driving test first time, and she now did some of the driving in the MG. Greg was very protective of that car so the guys knew Hannah must be a good driver. The TEAM were deployed on various jobs over the months but Greg had refused any contracts in December. They all needed a break and Harry, the only married member, could do with quality time with his family. Tim and Legs joined Sepp and Jack on a contract where an Arab businessman needed protection from potential kidnappers. The job lasted six weeks and was completed much to the Arabs satisfaction. He promised to refer his family and friends to the TEAM.

Harry reported that the music for the wedding was arranged, he'd mixed it himself, but refused any further information. Greg was secretly worried; his TEAM were pranksters and he was concerned at the possible content. He had no need to worry though.

As the day approached, and the banns were read, Greg, Hannah and the TEAM all attended church each Sunday. Katy Jones was a lively Dean, in her late forties. She had an infectious smile and they all warmed to her. The couple decided not to have stag and hen nights, simply inviting the TEAM, Jenny, Dickie and Sue, as well as Conner and his new girlfriend, Sofja, to stay over the weekend before the wedding.

When Conner arrived, Sav threw himself at the lad, wagging his tail ferociously, before rolling over to allow Conner to rub his stomach. The dog took to Sofja quickly and was soon darting between Hannah and Sofja, looking for attention. Eventually, Greg ordered him to stop and lie down. Everyone laughed at the dogs' facial expression. His head went down onto his huge paws, and his eyes looked around sadly, trying to get sympathy. When Sofja and Hannah sat talking on a settee, Greg allowed Sav to sit with them. Tim made the comment,

"Young Hannah has that dog eating out of her hands boss. You too mate!"

Greg smiled, "Too bloody true, mate"

The weekend went well, Dickie and Sue staying in a local hotel, and Jenny in the house. It was a very casual time, no airs and graces from anyone.

Soon enough, the day of the wedding came around. Hannah stayed the previous night at Tracey's, and Sofja joined them to help prepare for the big day.

On the night before, Conner and Harry sat in the conservatory. Conner had noticed his father had been quiet all day, taking himself off for walks around the estate. Harry advised leaving his boss alone.

"He's thinking mate. Just before a wedding, men do that. He's thinking if he's doing the right thing. He is, he just needs to work that out for himself. He's your dad, he loves you to bits. He'd die for you, but now he has someone else he'd die for. I know you are happy for him."

Conner looked at Harry.

"Yes, I get that. He's been my rock for so long. I'm so pleased he's happy, but for how long? Dad went through some serious shit when Miriam was murdered. I can't bear to see him go through that again. It'll break him, Harry, honest it will!"

Harry said nothing. All he could do was see that the day went according to plan. And safely.

The day of the wedding arrived. Greg dressed in his black Tuxedo outfit; tails included. His shirt was brushed white silk, and he sported a white bow tie. Conner wore an identical outfit, the pair looked impressive. Guests started arriving at the house and Greg was reliant on Harry to tell him the order of the day. The gate guard allowed those he knew in, without much trouble. The General, resplendent in his uniform, and Sue, looking gorgeous in a satin blue dress, arrived first. Sav greeted them enthusiastically, much to Dickie's chagrin. Harry and the TEAM arrived, suited and booted, and ready for action. Greg, after his walk, was calm.

"Ladies and Gents. Thank you for assembling here today. I'd rather walk in front of a firing squad than this. But" he added, "Today is the best day of my life. I would like to raise a glass to one who can't be with us. She'd have been impressed. I give you, 'Miriam'!"

Glasses were raised and chinked but the atmosphere was somewhat sombre. Then Greg announced,

"No Reception as such, but the pub is ours for the day! And, the drinks, Legs, are on ME!"

Legs laughed, "Can you afford me, Boss?" he asked.

Greg chuckled, "I'll drink you under any table you like, young man! And you know I can do it!"

Legs agreed, raising his glass,

"Yes, Greg, you bloody can, but, remember, it's your wedding night. Don't want to disappoint the Bride, eh?"

All laughed.

Greg was standing, staring out of the conservatory window, when he saw a white stretch Limo, a Mercedes, glide up the track. That must be his ride to the church, he was impressed. He went outside and watched as the driver skilfully parked by the door. 'Must be ex RCT' Greg thought and then did a double take as the driver stepped out.

"By all that's Holy!" he exclaimed. "John? John fecking Kelly? What, I mean, how did you know?"

John Kelly had served in the Royal Corps of Transport with Greg for years. They were great friends but had lost touch after Miriam had been killed.

"You can thank Harry!" John said, his broad Scottish accent

coming out loud and proud, and he continued, "Congratulations mate. By the way, the Limo is my wedding pressie to ye!"

They embraced, both with tears of joy in their eyes.

"Thanks mate. You will never know how much this means to me." Greg said quietly. "Has Harry…"

"Oh aye" John said, "He's briefed me, dinnae worry. You just relax. Oh, and by the way, Joseph sends his congratulations and says thanks."

Greg was lost for a moment, then remembered the failed sniper attack.

"How is he?" he asked.

"He's fine. New identity etc. He's my cousin. Did ye know that?" Greg shook his head. "Aye, well, he and I are very grateful. He won't be here but he says he'll be close. Just in case. You've made a good friend there."

Greg stepped into the car, along with Harry. Sepp sat up front, alongside John. Greg turned to Harry,

"You are full of surprises mate. I can't thank you enough." Harry chuckled,

"You ain't seen nothing yet!" he said, winking.

Hannah stood looking in the mirror. She sighed. Whilst she knew she looked beautiful, there was something missing. Something old, something new, something borrowed, something blue. She checked. New? The engagement ring, and soon a wedding band. Borrowed? The diamond and gold earrings Tracey had loaned her. Blue? That was the ribbon delicately tied to each shoe, but it was the 'something old' she struggled with. She mentioned it to Sofja, who, she had discovered, came from Novi Sad, in Serbia. Her English was perfect with just a hint of an accent.

"You have nothing old?" Sofja said. Hannah shook her head, sadly.

"But you will soon have Greg!" Sofja said, chuckling, "If he's like his son, he will appreciate the joke, I am thinking!" Hannah saw the funny side and hugged her new friend.

"Yes, I think he will! Thank you!"

Harry had made the arrangements for her as well as for Greg, so she had no idea what her transport would be. When Tracey called her to come downstairs, she was apprehensive. Her dress was in Ivory, mostly lace with a silk underskirt. It was halter neck and fairly revealing above the waist. She wore no bra and the dress maker had spared her any blushes by making the lace cover her breasts. The skirt fell gracefully to the floor and covered her Ivory shoes. She had a pearl necklace around her neck, and her hair, including extensions, had been turned into ringlets that fell to her shoulder blades. The blonde streaks had been emphasised to show off the tactful makeup. She looked, and felt, gorgeous. She descended the stairs and stepped out into the late winter sun. What she saw, took her breath away.

In the car park stood an old Army Green Goddess fire engine, complete with blue light and ladders. A soldier from the Royal Logistics Corps stood in best Blues, holding the door open.

"Oh my God!" she exclaimed. "It's, well, it's amazing!"

Tracey led her to the vehicle and helped her up, ensuring the dress remained immaculate. Tracey and Sofja would be following, in an old Austin 1800 Bomb Disposal car, again, complete with blue lights. They set off and, as they passed through the village, people looked, smiled and waved. The RLC driver treated them to a blast of the two-tone horn as they drove. Hannah giggled and waved enthusiastically. The Bomb Disposal car also saluted the villagers with sirens and lights.

The journey to Bangor took twenty minutes. As they approached, a police officer stopped traffic to let them through.

In the Cathedral, Greg paced nervously. All of the invited guests were assembled, there was much chatter. He heard the sirens but took no notice. Then there was a silence before Harry coughed, loudly. Greg had noticed a large television screen at the front of the building, behind the pulpit. It suddenly lit up and the scene from outside was displayed on it. A Green Goddess followed by a Bomb Disposal car pulled up and Hannah stepped out. Greg gasped.

"Harry!" he said, "How the feck did you manage that?"

Harry simply smiled. "The General pulled a few strings, mate."

As the Bride walked towards the entrance, music came from the speakers surrounding the church. Greg looked stunned. Instead of the usual Wedding March, the music played was "Beautiful Dream" sung by George Ezra. Greg looked stunned as the beautiful bride entered the church, accompanied by Tim. Greg remained facing forward, too scared to look around. He sensed Hannah move next to him and, contrary to protocol, laid her head on his shoulder.

"You old romantic, you!" she whispered, although most of the congregation heard!

Greg whispered back,

"Less of the old!" and the wedding guests laughed. The Dean took the ceremony which, afterwards, neither Greg nor Hannah, could remember. They both answered in the right places, sang the hymns when needed but were in a world of their own. At the words,

"You may now kiss the bride" they embraced and kissed briefly, both somewhat embarrassed. Greg started to turn and walk away with his new wife, but Harry stopped them.

"Have a look at the screen." he said. They turned back and saw on the screen, two singers they both adored, Matt and

Savannah Shaw. Greg gasped.

"NO!" he said, "It's a recording."

Then Savannah spoke,

"Hi, Greg and Hannah, and no, it's not a recording. We wanted to watch your wedding, which Harry has broadcast to the US especially for us. We're so happy for you, probably our greatest fans." Matt then spoke up,

"Sorry we couldn't make the wedding guys; Harry did invite us but we're recording an album. Anyway, we'd like to sing you down the aisle."

Greg looked hard at Harry. "You invited our favourite singers? Really?"

He heard Savannah chuckle,

"We'd love to have come to the UK. But, our present to you both is this." And she nodded at her father.

Matt and Savannah Shaw had burst onto the internet a few months earlier and were an instant hit with people worldwide, but especially Greg and Hannah. Their music was never far from whatever they were doing, and they idolised the Daddy and Daughter duo. For Harry to have arranged this was more than the icing on the cake. Hannah and Greg stood staring at the screen and the music started playing and the singing flowed into the church.

The song chosen was "The Prayer" which made both the

Bride and Groom look at each other, then at Harry, who simply winked. Then the newlyweds started walking slowly down the aisle, hand in hand accepting the many congratulations, and, as they reached the main entrance, the singing finished. Both turned and waited for the song to finish. The congregation applauded loudly and waved at the Daddy and Daughter Duo. Greg and Hannah also waved and thanked them.

"Thank you!" they both called and Matt and his beautiful daughter waved back. "You're welcome" they called back and the screen went blank. Hannah turned to Greg and said,

"No one has had a better wedding. I know that. Thank you, husband. I love you" and they kissed.

Once outside, they were greeted by John Kelly who poured them a glass of champagne and waved them to the limo. Hand in hand, surrounded by the TEAM, they climbed aboard. Cameras clicked and whirred, and the video camera Jack was in charge of swept the assembled people. As the car drove off, a motorbike rider watched with interest. The bike was a Harley Davidson Evo Softail. Manufactured in 1986 and kept in excellent condition, it boasted an air cooled, 4 stroke V Twin engine, it was painted in Candy Red with Gold lettering. It had cost Albana £20k and she used it to it's max. The rider smiled behind her tinted visor. She mentally toasted the bride and groom.

"Congratulations" she muttered, darkly. "For now!"

Chapter 28.

"New beginnings, and one ending"

The wedding limo was overtaken by the guests as they rushed to arrive at the reception before the newlyweds. Hannah and Greg sat chatting softly in the back, while John and Jack were up front. Tim and the rest followed in Greg's Landrover. They were alert. Jack sat reviewing the video he had recorded and paused the screen at one particular place. He stared at what he saw and cursed. Then he made a decision.

"John, pull over mate." John slowed and indicated to the left. Tim followed suit. Jack looked into the back and smiled,

"Nothing to worry about, Greg. Just need to swap cars. I need to sort this video camera out before the reception is ruined." And, saying that he jumped out of the car and ran back to where Tim and the others sat, waiting.

"Guys, listen, trust me. Legs, go in the limo. Take the long route, I'll explain later. Say nothing to the happy couple, ok?"

Legs climbed out and joined Greg and Hannah. Jack sat in the front of the Landrover and the small convoy started its journey again. Jack explained what he had seen to the others.

None were armed but that could soon change. Tim kept a watchful eye on his mirrors, looking in particular, for a red and burgundy, Harley Davidson motorbike. They devised a plan of action for when they arrived at the pub. Having been in this exact scenario many times, they each knew their role. Once Greg and Hannah were safely inside the venue, Tim would go to their house and collect small arms. They were ready to go to war to protect two of their own.

In the limo, Greg was asking why they were taking a longer route. Legs was a quick thinker,

"To give all the guests time to arrive before you, boss" he said, "Can't have you getting there first, can we?"

Greg nodded but wasn't convinced. He let it ride, thinking some sort of prank was about to befall them. As they approached the car park, Greg saw the invited guests assembled waiting for them. They left the car to applause and confetti being thrown over them. The Landrover pulled in after them and the guys quickly got out and formed a protective shield around Greg and Hannah. No one suspected anything. Photos were taken by the private photographer, and the couple went down onto the platform of the steam railway for more. A train arrived at the same time and the passengers, expecting to just see Santa, had an unexpected thrill, a wedding. Santa left the train and posed with the happy couple, although Tim had taken him aside and frisked him first.

"No offence, Santa, just being careful" he said, smiling. Greg was noticing what was happening and decided there was no prank coming, but something more serious. He switched on and became ultra-alert. He called Tim over,

"Are you nipping back to the house mate?" Tim nodded, not surprised that Greg had cottoned on.

"Then bring me one. And bring Sav." Tim again nodded, understanding. He went to the Landrover and drove off. The TEAM stayed alert, looking for the motorbike but there was no sign. Jack wondered if he'd been too quick to suspect, but trusted his instincts. While the photo shoot was taking place, Legs and Sepp had entered the pub, checking surreptitiously for anything untoward. Ten minutes later, Tim returned and they went into the back room and passed around pistols. Sav sat quietly. Tim had put him 'on guard' which meant the dog would ignore all those he knew but be suspicious of anyone else. The guys then checked the main reception room carefully. Tracey noticed and called Tim over.

"What's up, Tim?" she asked. He smiled,

"Just us boys making sure everything is ready, Trace, nothing to worry about." Then the guys formed a guard of honour outside the main entrance and clapped Greg and Hannah as they went inside. Sav sat just inside, ears up, highly alert. Jack and Sepp remained outside while the others went through to the reception room. Champagne corks popped, and the chatter became louder. Greg excused himself from his new wife and went to speak to Tim who explained what they suspected. Greg cursed,

"Albana? The bitch. Where's my pistol?" Tim passed it to him, checking to make sure no one could see. "It's loaded, one in the breech, safety on." Greg nodded, "Thanks mate." And returned to Hannah who had not noticed anything.

A little over three miles away, in a small layby near a forest, Albana sat astride her bike. She took a package from one of the panniers and checked it. The large padded envelope contained an improvised explosive device. It had been made for her by a former IRA bomb maker. He had shown her how to prime it and she was almost ready. She was waiting until she was sure the wedding party was inside before going to the pub and throwing the bomb through a window. She glanced at her watch and decided it was time to move. She glanced over her shoulder and pulled onto the road. Coming towards her was a Suzuki Grand Vitara. Albana took no notice, merely concentrating on throwing the bomb. Suddenly, the Vitara swerved and slammed into her bike, head on, at over fifty miles an hour. The impact sent her flying through the air, landing on the top of her head, almost sixty metres away. Her neck snapped with a loud crack and she died on impact with the tarmac road. The Vitara stopped and the driver ran back. There was no other traffic on the road. The driver checked the rider's pulse. She was dead and he smiled. He picked up the envelope and ran back to his car, quickly looked at the damage to the bonnet before driving off swiftly. Three miles along the road, parked in a layby which could not be seen from the main road, was a 7.5-ton car transporter, with ramps down from the tailgate. The curtains on the sides were sealed tight. The driver drove into the back and climbed out. Another man packed away the ramps and closed the rear doors. He took the bomb from the car driver and drove away. Joseph then got into his own car and drove to the pub, but took a longer route. John was waiting outside. They shook hands and Joseph explained quickly what had happened, and why. Just then, they saw Tim approaching.

"Seems there's been a terrible accident, Tim" Joseph said. "Seems a female motorbike rider has been killed in a hit and run. Tell Greg thanks, favour returned." And with that he left. John updated Tim who got the TEAM together and told them the news. Pistols were handed back and Tim took them, and Sav, back to the house. Greg was relieved but also saddened that it had come to this. A woman who was trying to kill him and Hannah had lost her life needlessly. The event cast a shadow over his day but he tried to put it behind him. He would tell Hannah later, but for now, the reception would carry on.

An abundant buffet had been laid on by Tracey and Greg and Hannah tucked in, both starving. They circulated, holding hands, happy to greet people, but both keen to be alone. After a while, they went outside and smoked a cigarette. People passing greeted them and smiled. All was well. They saw a police car and an ambulance passing, blue lights and sirens on the go. Hannah sighed,

"Oh I hope no one is badly injured, not on this, our happiest day." Greg said nothing, just imagining the scene further down the road. After a few minutes, Conner and Sofja joined them, holding hands. Greg smiled, his son had found a beautiful, intelligent and loving partner. He shook hands and hugged his son, then turned to Sofja,

"Sofja, I'm sorry to announce that Conner is indeed my son! Despite being taller and better looking than me, he really is my son." They all chuckled. Sofja spoke quietly,

"Greg, he has all of your finer attributes. I'm proud to have met him and you. But especially happy to have met Hannah. You make a wonderful couple."

Greg blushed and Hannah hugged Sofja. Then they went inside as, Conner reminded his father, Greg had a speech to make.

While the wedding reception was in full swing, the North Wales Police Accident Investigation Team were at the scene of the fatal collision. The NWP AIT were extremely experienced and had no trouble identifying the nature of the collision. A witness reported seeing a red Suzuki Grand Vitara driving away, it had front damage and the witness had captured it on his dashcam. The speed of the two vehicles was such that the driver of the Vitara was not clear on the screen. Sergeant Huw Edwards reported this to Control, who told him to await a call from Manchester. Edwards was puzzled but waited patiently. The call came through very quickly. Detective Inspector 'Gore' Downey had placed a marker which stated that, any incidents within a ten-mile radius of Greg's house, was to be referred to him. He obtained the facts from Edwards and asked the identity of the victim. When he heard it was Albana Flaka, he swore softly.

"Sergeant, get round to Greg Angels house, it's Llamedos, in the village. Check where he was at the time of this crash. Then call me back as soon as possible. I'll be waiting!"

Sergeant Edwards sent a patrol car to the house, but they returned saying that Greg was in the pub, only three miles down the road, at his wedding reception. Edwards relayed that to Gore. His next instruction was simple. Go to the pub and question everyone there. Edwards and his team set off, still puzzled as to what this crash had to do with Manchester police.

The speeches over, it was time for the newly weds first dance. Greg had no idea what he would be dancing to and asked Hannah. She simply smiled,

"I chose it, don't worry." Greg relaxed. The pair moved onto the dance floor and waited. Hannah held Greg close and rested her head on his shoulder as the first notes played. Greg held her tight and kissed the top of her head as 'I won't last a day without you' by the Carpenters played.

"How did you know?" he asked.

"I flicked through your cd collection the other night and told Harry. The words seemed to fit. I hope you like it?"

Greg kissed her again, "Like it? I love it. You are so thoughtful, thank you." They moved slowly together, lost in their own bubble. Gradually, other couples joined them and Greg was pleased to see Tim embracing Tracey. The two men smiled at each other and Greg whispered to Hannah,

"I think there'll be another wedding soon"

Hannah agreed but was more than happy to continue the dance for as long as possible. Their mood was interrupted by the arrival of three police officers at the door. A Sergeant spoke to Legs and looked directly at Greg who uncoupled himself from his wife and walked over.

"Can we help you, Sergeant?" he asked.

"Mr Angel?" was the stern reply.

"Yes, what is wrong?"

"There has been a fatal road collision three miles along the road to Beddgelert. Wondered if you knew anything about it?"

Greg shook his head as Hannah joined him,

"What happened?" he asked.

"A motorbike, containing one person, the rider, was struck head on in a hit and run accident. The rider suffered fatal injuries. She has been taken to the hospital morgue." The

Sergeant was being as harsh as he could get away with and noted the look on the bride's face. It was one of sheer horror, obvious that she had no knowledge of the accident. He was, however, concerned with the look of total disinterest on Greg's face. Hannah asked the question,

"Do you know who she is?"

"A foreign national, name of Albana Flaka." Came the response. Hannah gasped and Edwards seized the opportunity,

"A friend of yours madam?" he asked. Hannah looked confused and Greg took over,

"We met her once, that's all. What is this to us?"

"Well Sir, a Detective Inspector Downey from Greater Manchester Police, had put a marker on this area. For some reason, any incident in a ten-mile radius of your house was to be reported to him. Now why would that be?"

Greg smiled, a move that the Sergeant spotted.

"Ah, 'Gore' Downey. No Sergeant, we have no idea."

Edwards then turned to the guests,

"Do any of you own, or drive, a Red Suzuki Grand Vitara?"

They all shook their head and it was at this point that Jenny stepped in,

"Sergeant, may I have a word, in private?"

Edwards had no idea who she was but saw a professional woman and so agreed. They went outside and Jenny produced her identity card.

"Military Intelligence, Sergeant. You can rest assured that the incident you are investigating has nothing to do with anybody here. Please inform Downey that I will be speaking to him at a later date. Now then, you may return to your duties." With that she walked back into the bar and beckoned Greg, Hannah and Tim over,

"We need to talk! And NOW! I want the facts please."

They walked outside, over the footbridge and onto the railway platform, the only place where secrecy was guaranteed. Greg told her what they knew, which was precious little. She nodded and spoke quietly and calmly.

"This means that Flaka hasn't given up." Hannah looked shocked, Greg and Tim had a determined look on their faces and it was Greg who spoke.

"Jenny, find out where this bastard is right now! I intend putting this to a stop. My wife and I will be in the bar, having a celebratory drink, when you find out, tell me!" He took Hannah by the arm and led the way, Tim trailing behind. Inside, the atmosphere was subdued so Tim made an announcement,

"Nothing to see here folks! DJ, get some music on and everyone drink up!"

Then he went to Greg,

"What are you planning boss?" he asked, "And whatever it is, you are not, I repeat not, doing it alone. I hope I make myself clear?"

Greg eyed his friend and nodded,

"Volunteers only Tim, I hope I make *myself* clear?"

Tim nodded, "Seven volunteers then!"

Greg sighed and Hannah took his hand, "That includes me, Husband. We're together, always will be, so don't even think about leaving me out. In a way, I started this, I'm damned well going to help end it!" Greg looked into her beautiful blue eyes and nodded,

"But I apply the coup de grace, ok?"

Seconds later, Jenny returned.

"Flaka is at his villa in Greece, Halkidiki to be precise. I want to know what you plan Greg!"

"Best you don't know, Jenny" he replied, "Is Boumby still in Athens?"

Jenny started.

"You can not be fucking serious Greg! You can't go steaming into Greece, commit murder and hope to get out alive?"

"Murder? Why would I murder him? He might simply have an accident, a gas leak or something. Look Jenny, if I don't go there and confront him this will never end. For fucks sake, it's our wedding day and the bastard sent his daughter to kill us! With an explosive device which could have killed or injured many more. You think I should let him try again? No, get a phone number for him. I'm going to call him and invite him to meet me, alone. Let me know when you've got it."

Jenny waved her iPhone, "Here it is. You're a stubborn bastard Angel but I can read your mind. Call him now, on loudspeaker so we can all hear." The small group moved outside and Greg hit the dial button. The ring tone told him he was indeed calling a European number. It rang a few times before a gruff voice answered,

"Angel you murdering bastard! She was my only daughter!"

Greg spoke softly,

"You sent your daughter, Flaka. I had nothing to do with her death, believe that or not, I don't care. Now listen you piece of shit, I'm coming over. You can meet me, one to one, if you have the guts. Just remember this, sooner or later, everyone sits down to a banquet of consequences. You are about to be force fed! I'll call you when I arrive."

He terminated the call, his anger threatening to burst forth. Hannah touched him lightly, stroking his arm, feeling the tension trickle through his shirt, until, as quickly as it arrived, the tension left him. Jenny nodded,

"Alright, I'll book a flight for one." Hannah spoke up,

"Seven flights, Jenny. Understood?" Jenny glared at this girl but agreed, "Ok, seven flights. If I don't see any of you again, it's been nice knowing you." With that she walked off, shoulders slumped, doubt about Greg's return filling her head.

Greg turned to the others,

"Hannah, we have a dance to finish. Tim, tell the others what you and Hannah have volunteered them for. I'll call a halt to the party shortly, in respect of a deceased biker. Then we go home, plan and prepare. I'll call Boumby. Anything we need, he'll supply. Let's go, oh and Tim, for fuck sake, when we get back, marry Tracey will you?"

Hannah stopped Greg before they returned to the reception.

"Who is Boumby?" she asked. Greg smiled,

"Boumby is an ex Greek Navy Petty Officer. He's a fixer. He can supply anything we, sorry, I need whilst out there. I've known him from my holidays in Greece. He's one of the good guys. You'll like him."

The couple then went back to their celebration. However, he made the announcement and the party ended early. Conner looked concerned;, he knew his father well. Greg reassured him,

"It doesn't seem right, mate, that this party should continue after such a tragedy." Conner agreed and, when he and Sofja left to drive home, he hugged his Dad and whispered,

"Safe, Father, safe. OK?" Greg nodded and waved his son goodbye, arm in arm with his new wife. Pride flooded through him, not just because he was now married to the woman he loved, but because his son was intuitive.

Chapter 29.

"Between a rock, and a hard face."

'Gore' Downey took the call from Sergeant Edwards and growled. The update was not what he wanted to hear. Angel must have been involved, but some woman from Military Intelligence had interfered. Wedding or not, Angel either had a hand in Albana's death or he knew what happened. He told Edwards to keep the incident under wraps for now. He sat in his lounge, a glass of Bushmills in hand, thinking of his next move.

He decided and called his opposite number in Bangor CID. They chatted and 'Gore' persuaded the Inspector to put a watch on Greg's house. However, due to manpower shortages, it wouldn't be in place until nine o'clock next morning. 'Gore' had to accept that and carried on with his Bushmills.

The flight to Athens was to leave Manchester Airport at 09.05 next day. It entailed one stop, at Schiphol Airport, Amsterdam, with a lay over of over four hours. Arrival at Athens was 16.35, local time.

It was far from ideal but Greg could do nothing about it. He bought seven business class tickets and gulped at the price. They decided to take hand luggage only and Boumby had arranged to meet them with two hire cars, BMW X5's, in black. The journey from Athens to Polichrono was more than six hundred kilometres, a drive of about seven hours. They would share the driving, except Hannah who had never driven abroad before. The flight to Schiphol was uneventful. The team had arrived at Manchester over two hours early and settled in. A common expression in the army is 'hurry up and wait' and the veterans were prepared. Hannah was less so and was restless until the plane took off. Then she settled and opened her Kindle to do a bit of light reading. She had downloaded one of Harry's books, 'Harry was a Crap Hat' and, during the flight, she found herself chuckling out loud. Harry looked over and smiled. She caught his eye and said,

"I thought you didn't like fiction, Harry?" He laughed, "Every word in there is true Hannah. And Greg doesn't get one mention!"

When they arrived at Amsterdam, they went to eat and have a beer. Just the one though. They watched their surroundings but were confident they were not being watched.

An unmarked car sat down the track from Llamedos, two plain clothes police inside. They'd arrived at just before nine o'clock and had called at the house. The security guard on the gate had refused them entry and also refused to give them information, not opening the electric gate. They moved off to a distance, plainly in sight. It was going to be a long wait!

Finally the TEAM boarded their flight to Athens, arriving at 16.30 local. Greg stretched his legs and Hannah packed her Kindle away. All seven were apprehensive but made their way through customs with no problem. Ostensibly they were a darts team, playing in a tournament in Thessaloniki. As they walked to arrivals, Greg saw Boumby. If anything, he'd put on more weight than Greg remembered. They embraced and Greg did the introductions. The Greek took them to their hired cars and climbed into the driving seat of one. Greg spoke,

"Boumby, I can't involve you mate."

"Greg, I am already involved. These cars and the other items you requested; I supply. And I want to be able to return them when this is over. Anyway, an extra driver will be good, no?"

Greg couldn't argue with that and so they climbed into the cars, Greg, Hannah and Tim with Boumby, the others in the rear vehicle. Tim sat up front, he didn't trust Greeks! The group drove all night, with only one stop for toilet break and refreshments. Hannah was stunned at the number of tolls they had to pass through. Her sight of Greece was marred by the darkness, but she was pleased that the temperature was quite high, for the time of year. Hardly a word was spoken. Hannah looked outside but saw very little. Eventually, just after midnight, the convoy arrived in the sleepy village of Polichrono. Out of season, the village held just 300 residents. Most restaurants were closed and it was a ghost town. As they pulled up at their hotel, a man in police uniform stepped from the shadows and waved them to stop. Tim cursed, "Shit!"

Greg patted his back,

"Relax, that's Makis, the local Chief of Police. We have history but it's all cool." He stepped out of the car and shook the officer's hand. There was a short conversation in Greek and money changed hands. Greg beckoned the rest to follow him and bring their bags. The Summer Dream Hotel was a modern building in the traditional Greek style. At this time of night, it was dark except for emergency lighting. The hotel was just 100 yards from the beach and the group were allocated three rooms on the top of three floors. Each room opened onto a balcony with a fine view over the peninsula, Sithonia facing them, deeply dark. Greg told Hannah that the third Peninsula was called Athos and the Peninsula they were on was called Kassandra. Boumby had left the TEAM with Makis who invited them to supper in the restaurant on the ground floor. The owner of the hotel, Viktoria Tallos had prepared various meats, with salad and Retsina on hand. Viktoria was a beautiful, vivacious Hungarian woman and knew Greg from previous visits. They hugged and Hannah was embraced as well.

"Congratulations, Mrs Angel!" Viktoria said, "He's good man. A little wild at times but he has a heart of pure gold." Hannah laughed,

"Wild? Oh I hope so!"

The TEAM sat at one table and discussed what was going to happen. Makis informed them that Granit and Ismet were the only other staff at Flaka's villa. Greg decided to carry out a recce in the early hours, under the cover of darkness. He had planned to telephone Flaka the next morning but decided to wait. His adversary might send his thugs into the village and would report strangers in town. While they ate, Makis reminded Greg of an incident when he had been on holiday there. Turning to Hannah he spoke quietly,

"A few years ago, when Mr Greg was on holiday here, a lady and her two daughters were walking past a restaurant. Two dogs decided to have a fight and ran in among the lady's legs. The mother, she screamed and Mr Greg heard. He ran from his apartment, picked up the two snarling dogs and threw them away. The dogs were so shocked, they ran off. The lady was very happy and thanked Mr Greg. He simply walked away. The lady was from Serbia and she wanted to thank Mr Greg properly. Her two daughters, Sofja and Aleksandra were also very grateful, being so young it had shocked them. Mr Greg, he had a meal with them. Then, an Albanian was being nasty to the Mother who, you must understand, was a great beauty, and she told Mr

Greg. Mr Greg, he watched and saw this man calling obscene comments to the lady. So, Mr Greg, he came to me with a choice, he deals with this man, or I could. I decided to act and the Albanian was deported the next day. Mr Greg left the day after. Mr Greg helped many people out whenever he was on holiday here. He has a great many friends. He won't talk about this much, but he has an English sense of fair play and we respect him for this." Hannah looked at her husband and could imagine him being so gallant. Then her heart leapt. Sofja? No, surely not, that must be a common name in Serbia. She vowed to ask Conner's girlfriend later.

As two a.m. arrived, Makis took Greg to one side. When the pair returned, Hannah had to look twice. Greg was dressed in the uniform of a Greek Policeman, complete with pistol on his belt. He also wore the regulation cap. He and Makis strolled casually away from the hotel, in the opposite direction to the villa. The TEAM remained in the restaurant which was now in darkness. Tim was worried,

"I don't like this" he said in his West Country drawl, "We've no weapons if anything erupts. Don't seem right." It was Hannah who replied,

"Greg can handle himself as you well know, Tim. And to any outsider, it's just two Greek cops doing a last patrol."

Tim nodded and kept quiet. This girl had developed a sensible head and he appreciated that. The whole TEAM would die for her and Greg, and he just hoped that would not be necessary.

'Gore' Downey was furious.

"What the fuck do you mean, 'as far as you know, he's still inside'? Get in there to find out!" he shouted down the phone. The Inspector told him that, without a warrant, there was nothing he could do. 'Gore' stormed out of his office and along to his Chief Constable. After explaining the situation, a warrant was issued for the arrest of Greg Angel and his TEAM on suspicion of terrorist offences. 'Gore' smiled, "gotcha!" After emailing the warrant 'Gore' sat down to wait. If Angel wasn't there at least they could search the house.

Greg and Makis walked slowly around the streets, passing closed hotels, silent apartments, hearing only the barking of foxes scavenging for food, eventually ending up behind the villa. The lighting around the building showed three storeys, walls of white alabaster with brick pillars at each corner. The roof was of traditional Roman tiles and there were four chimneys. Keeping to the shadows, the pair strolled towards the beach. The sand was bone dry and as fine as dust. No lights shone on the beach; all lights shone inwards to the house. There were palm trees and one old orange tree and the grass was green and well-watered. There was no sign of life inside. They stopped under an awning, both lighting cigarettes. This was partly a bluff, anyone with evil intent would do no such thing. It also gave Greg time to study the building and formulate a plan. The wall and fence surrounding the premises was brick pillars with wire stretched in between. At the top was military razor wire. Greg had seen enough and they returned to the hotel, creeping in so quietly they made the others jump. Greg laughed,

"Good job you haven't got weapons or I'd be dead now." He sat and poured himself a glass of Retsina. After telling them of the security of the building he made a decision.

"It's plan B. I call that Albanian bastard tomorrow and challenge him to meet me on his beach, it's fairly dark and secluded. There we will settle this once and for all."

Hannah stared at him, then ran from the room and upstairs to their room. They could all hear her sobs and no-one looked at Greg. They all felt terrible for the girl. Newly married and tomorrow evening, she could well be a widow. One by one, they left the restaurant and went to their own rooms. Not one bade Greg a goodnight. Makis sighed,

"Malaka, you are crazy. Good night." And also left. Greg had a cigarette before going upstairs, filled with trepidation. Hannah lay face down on the double bed, still crying. He sat beside her, saying nothing. After a while, she turned over to look at him, her eyes red with tears. She threw her arms around him and held tight.

"Don't do it, please!" she begged, fear in her voice. Her took her face in his hands,

"My dear darling. I married you because I love you. But I must ask, do you think I would do this if I didn't think, or even know the outcome. Tomorrow night, we'll make use of that pool out there and I'll drink Retsina. Have faith."

Hannah looked at him and saw something she did not expect to see. A smile that held cunning deep down and she felt slightly better. 'He's going to shoot him!' she thought. 'That must be his Plan B, lure Flaka out then shoot him.' She kissed him and they lay together, cuddling and relaxing. They drifted off to sleep together.

Inspector Downey paced his office. He jumped as the phone rang and he snatched at it.

"Nothing? No people, no weapons? Nothing?" he roared into the phone. "For Fucks sake!" and he terminated the call. "Burrows!" he bellowed, "Get onto flight control, I want to know where that bastard has gone to!"

The TEAM awoke at sunrise the next morning which was just after seven thirty. Greg knew the sun would set at around five p.m. and made his plans. After breakfast, he sent Sepp and Jack, with sand coloured ghillie suits to the beach half a mile beyond the villa. They took a circular route via the hamlet of Hanioti, emerging onto the beach at the Alexander the Great Hotel, which was closed up. Both were armed with rifles and pistols, supplied by Boumby. Their instructions were to proceed along the beach in their Ghillies and settle near the villa, totally undercover. They had seven hours to get to their position. Legs took up a position in the building nearest the villa, a place called the Brit Bar. He was let into a room and settled with a sniper rifle. He'd never fired it but, at the distance of only fifty yards, he knew he could not miss. Tim and Greg discussed the plan of action. Hannah sat listening, scared more than ever before. Greg tried to sooth her but it had no effect. He felt really bad, as if he were deceiving her. He had a plan and knew that, if it failed, he'd be dead. At ten o'clock, he called Flaka. The Albanian chuckled when he answered,

"So, Englishman, you are here, yes?" Greg paused,

"I'm here. Five o'clock, on your little private beach. Just you and me. Your banquet of consequences is about to be served." And ended the call. Harry, Greg, Hannah and Tim sat by the pool, in silence. Tim found it difficult to look at his boss. He wanted to offer to fight the big Albanian but knew that Greg would never allow it to happen. They just had to wait and see.

At a quarter to five, Greg put a pistol in a holster on his belt and walked the main street to the beach, Hannah, Tim and Harry some fifty yards behind. Ahead of him he saw Flaka on the beach, loosening up and flexing his muscles. Granit stood one side and Ismet the other. Greg got nearer and Harry and Tim raised their rifles. Tim covered Granit and Harry covered Ismet. The sun was setting behind Greg, just as he had planned. He moved slowly, stopping roughly ten feet from Flaka. The

Albanian had stripped to the waist and his muscles rippled, emphasising the many tattoos. He sneered at Greg,

"As you can see Englishman, I have no weapon, only my strength. Throw your pistol away."

Greg unbuckled the belt slowly and passed it to Hannah,

"Any funny moves, shoot the bastard" he murmured. As he turned back, Granit and Ismet drew pistols and pointed them at Harry and Tim. Greg smiled,

"Can't trust you can we, Flaka?" he laughed. The next thing the two thugs felt were barrels resting on the back of their necks and the instruction, "drop your weapons!"

They did so and Flaka stepped forward, towards Greg, leaving roughly six feet between them. That suited Greg. The sun was warm on his back and he waited. No one moved, no one spoke. The tension could be cut with a knife. A minute passed, Tim and the others waiting for something to happen, and then Greg was ready. He noticed Flaka squint as the sun, setting over Greg's shoulder, blinded him. Greg knelt down, scooped up a large stone before leaping high into the air and bringing the stone down on the Albanian's bald head. The sound was like a clap of thunder and Hannah felt sick. Flaka's skull split inside and, technically, he was dead. He just didn't know it. Greg landed on both feet and watched. Confusion, pain and hate filled the face of his enemy, but he remained standing. Greg feared he had not hit Flaka hard enough and stepped forward, delivering a tremendous punch to the man's nose. Flaka swayed, his eyes closing, then he toppled backwards, arms outstretched and lifeless. Granit and Ismet stood stunned and awaited their execution as some five guns were pointed at them. Greg stepped in front of Granit and head butted him. He fell, out cold. Ismet tried to run but was held by a fast- moving Tim. Hannah stepped forward, drawing her pistol. Greg made no attempt to stop her as she lashed the pistol grip across Ismet's nose. He screamed with pain and fell to his knees. Jack slapped Granit back to life and pushed him alongside his brother. Greg stood before them.

"Your boss is dead. You, at present, are not. The villa is that way. Take what you want and leave. If I ever see you again, Hannah here will knee cap you before killing you. Do you understand?"

The twins nodded and staggered to the villa. Hannah holstered her pistol and turned to Greg.

As if out of nowhere, four local fishermen appeared, picked up the lifeless body and dumped it into a boat, before pushing it out to sea. Makis explained that Flaka would be buried at sea, weighted down with rocks and chains, never to be seen again.

Hannah nodded then marched up to Greg. She stood on tiptoe, her face red with anger, looked him in the eyes and said,

"Husband, if you ever, ever, EVER scare me like that again, I'll fucking kneecap YOU!" before collapsing in his arms.

Slowly, the group walked back to the hotel. Outside, driving a battered old van, was Boumby. He took the weapons, hugged Greg and drove away, relieved that no shots had been fired. Legs patted Greg on the back.

"Fucking awesome, boss, fucking awesome!"

Half an hour later they sat around the pool. Greg had telephoned Jenny with only two words, 'situation resolved' and hung up. He badly needed a drink and so Viktoria brought a bottle of Kourtakis Retsina and set it before him. She patted his shoulder and winked at Hannah.

The TEAM demanded to know his tactics and so he explained.

"I knew Flaka would try something, that's why I had Jack and Sepp in cammo on the beach. I also knew he'd face this way; he knew where we were staying and the direction we would come from. He simply hadn't realised the sun would be in his face. Also, counting wasn't his strong point or he'd have noticed that three of us were nowhere to be seen. I knew the sun would be behind me and, at some point, he'd be blinded. When he squinted, that's when I took action. I was worried for a moment that I hadn't hit him hard enough, hence the punch. Plan B worked." He took a drink and sighed, before continuing,

"I'm so sorry Hannah, I couldn't say anything, in case it went tits up. Please forgive me?"

She took his hand and kissed it,

"I meant what I said though Greg. Never, ever do anything like that again."

Greg knew he couldn't promise that and so kept quiet.

At that moment, his mobile phone rang and he cursed.

"Hannah, would you get that please?" He had left his phone on the bar and Hannah walked over and picked it up. She listened, spoke a few words, glancing occasionally at Greg then ended the call. Her eyes filled with tears as she went back to her new family. Sitting down, she sobbed.

"I'm so sorry Greg, I'm so very sorry, that was Jenny. It's John. He's been murdered. Shot dead in Londonderry."

A stunned silence filled the air. Greg broke it,

"Flaka's last act of revenge?" he asked. Hannah looked at him, sorrow on her face.

"No Darling, she said it was a group called the Diverse IRA".

The End

Dedications.

I am dedicating this book to several people.

First, and foremost, to the real Hannah. Yes, she exists, and yes, the manner of our meeting is as detailed in the book. Hannah gave me the inspiration to write this novel, an adventure romance. Not my usual genre. I met Hannah and tried to help, but I failed. For that I am very sorry, but, if the real Hannah contacts me, paulreesauthor@gmail.com maybe I can change that failure into a success. I cannot guarantee that I could have promoted her like the fictional Hannah, but I'd have liked to try. I wish you well, Hannah.

I dedicate the book also, to those who loaned me their names, primarily Harry Clacy, a fellow author. Harry didn't read fiction, until I persuaded him to look at this book. Strangely, he was impressed! His books are available on Amazon. 'Harry was a Crap Hat' is a real book and, for veterans of the great Royal Corps of Transport, a valuable resource. And, no, I'm not in any of Harry's books!

Sepp and Jack are based on real characters too. Their background stories are factual. To a point.

Greg is based on a real character too. Sadly, not me. Sofja and Viktoria are very real. Both beautiful, intelligent and gorgeous people. I am proud to say Sofja calls me 'Uncle'. That is an accolade in itself. Viktoria calls me 'Pelican'. Now, that's another story!

The book cover was designed by Sharon Brownlie, c/o aspirebookcovers.com I am well pleased and will continue the trend with the sequels.

Some place names have been changed. Some are there today. Snowdonia is a fantastic place to live and visit.

I wish to thank Matt and Savannah Shaw. For their music and permission to use their names in the book. It is I who am honoured.

I hope you enjoyed 'Hannah, I am the storm'. Now to write the sequel, "Angel's Revenge" Thank you for reading.

If you have enjoyed this book, please leave a review on Amazon. We self-published authors thrive on reviews. When I started writing, in 2012, I wrote 'When we've said Goodbye' because I had a story to tell. It was a hobby. "Hannah" has been a labour of love. I will be putting a percentage of any profits from this book aside, in the hope that, one day, the real Hannah can benefit from it.

Printed in Great Britain
by Amazon